What if your friend was trapped in a painting?

Olive couldn't help thinking about Morton and his *other* friends while she climbed back into bed and settled Hershel beside her on the pillow. Even in her dreams, she saw Morton's face. She saw him standing before his huge, empty house, with no mother or father waiting inside. She watched him running through the misty fields, chasing a friend who wasn't there, while she was stuck on the outside of his world, with no way in.

She had to find that spellbook so that she could help Morton. She had to find some answers. And she had to find them *soon*.

OTHER BOOKS YOU MAY ENJOY

The Books of Elsewhere: Volume 1: The Shadows	Jacqueline West
Charlie and the Chocolate Factory	Roald Dahl
The Ghost's Grave	Peg Kehret
Island of the Aunts	Eva Ibbotson
The Ogre of Oglefort	Eva Ibbotson
Savvy	Ingrid Law
Scumble	Ingrid Law
The Secret of Platform 13	Eva Ibbotson
Small Persons with Wings	Ellen Booraem
Sophie's Mixed-Up Magic #1: Wishful Thinking	Amanda Ashby
A Tale Dark & Grimm	Adam Gidwitz
Which Witch?	Eva Ibbotson
The Witches	Roald Dahl

THE BOOKS OF
ELSEWHERE
volume two
SPELLBOUND

by Jacqueline West

illustrated by Poly Bernatene

PUFFIN BOOKS
An Imprint of Penguin Group (USA) Inc.

PUFFIN BOOKS

Published by the Penguin Group

Penguin Young Readers Group, 345 Hudson Street, New York, New York 10014, U.S.A.

Penguin Group (Canada), 90 Eglinton Avenue East, Suite 700, Toronto, Ontario, Canada M4P 2Y3
(a division of Pearson Penguin Canada Inc.)

Penguin Books Ltd, 80 Strand, London WC2R 0RL, England

Penguin Ireland, 25 St Stephen's Green, Dublin 2, Ireland (a division of Penguin Books Ltd)

Penguin Group (Australia), 250 Camberwell Road, Camberwell, Victoria 3124, Australia
(a division of Pearson Australia Group Pty Ltd)

Penguin Books India Pvt Ltd, 11 Community Centre,
Panchsheel Park, New Delhi - 110 017, India

Penguin Group (NZ), 67 Apollo Drive, Rosedale, Auckland 0632, New Zealand
(a division of Pearson New Zealand Ltd.)

Penguin Books (South Africa) (Pty) Ltd, 24 Sturdee Avenue,
Rosebank, Johannesburg 2196, South Africa

Registered Offices: Penguin Books Ltd, 80 Strand, London WC2R 0RL, England

First published in the United States of America by Dial Books for Young Readers,
a division of Penguin Young Readers Group, 2011
Published by Puffin Books, a division of Penguin Young Readers Group, 2012

1 3 5 7 9 10 8 6 4 2

Text copyright © Jacqueline West, 2011
Illustrations copyright © Poly Bernatene, 2011
All rights reserved

THE LIBRARY OF CONGRESS HAS CATALOGED THE DIAL EDITION AS FOLLOWS:
West, Jacqueline, date.
Spellbound / by Jacqueline West ; illustrated by Poly Bernatene.
p.   cm. — (The books of Elsewhere ; v. 2)
Sequel to: Shadows.
Summary: Eleven-year-old Olive finds herself drawn to the grimoire of the witches
who built her house and tries to use its spells to uncover the house's magic
and control the cats themselves, but the book is more wicked than it seems.
ISBN: 978-0-8037-3441-8 (hc)
[1. Space and time—Fiction. 2. Dwellings—Fiction. 3. Magic—Fiction.
4. Books and reading—Fiction. 5. Cats—Fiction.]
I. Bernatene, Poly, ill. II. Title.
PZ7.W51776Spe 2011
[Fic]—dc22 2010041865

Puffin Books ISBN 978-0-14-242102-4

Designed by Jennifer Kelly
Text set in Requiem

Printed in the United States of America

For Danny and Alex—
with ten thousand
good memories

—JW

THE BOOKS OF
ELSEWHERE

volume two

SPELLBOUND

EVERYONE WHO LIVED in the big stone house on Linden Street eventually went insane.

That was what the neighbors said, anyway. Mr. Fergus told Mr. Butler about Aldous McMartin, the house's first owner, a weird old artist who wouldn't sell a single painting and who only came out of the house at night. Mrs. Dewey and Mr. Hanniman whispered about Annabelle McMartin, Aldous's granddaughter, who had kicked the bucket right there inside the house at the age of 104, with no friends or family to notice she was dead except for her three gigantic cats, who may or may not have begun nibbling on her head.

And now there were these new owners—these Dunwoodys—who appeared to have already bought their tickets for the crazy train.

Since the beginning of the summer, the neighbors up and down Linden Street had gotten used to seeing a quiet, gangly girl playing or reading in the yard of the big stone house. The girl was usually alone, but every now and then a man with thick glasses and thin hair would mosey out, take the ancient push mower from the shed, and cut one or two crooked rows of grass before stopping to stare up at the sky and mutter to himself. Then he would rush back into the house, leaving the mower on the lawn. Sometimes the mower stood there for days.

At other times, a middle-aged woman came out of the house and wandered around the lawn, absently watering the weeds. The woman was also prone to leaving bags of groceries on the roof of her car, which sent bouncing cascades of oranges and onions down Linden Street each time she pulled out of the driveway. The neighbors watched all of this and shook their heads.

Then, on one bright July morning, the quiet, gangly girl walked out to the mailbox carrying two cans of paint. Behind her trotted a splotchily colored cat with a fishbowl over its head. The house loomed over them, its windows blank and dark, watching. While the cat waited, the girl stood on the curb and painted over the name *McMartin*, which was still scrawled along the side of the mailbox, and spelled out *DUNWOODY* on top of it in big green capitals.

Mrs. Nivens, who lived next door and who was pretending to spray her roses, kept a close watch on the pair. Her face was completely enclosed in the shade of her big-brimmed sunhat, but if anyone had gotten a good look at her, they would have seen that her eyes were sharp and interested.

"Ready to return from orbit?" Mrs. Nivens heard the girl whisper to the cat. "Preparing to reenter Earth's atmosphere in five, four, three, two . . ."

Both the cat and the girl sprang forward, charged up the porch steps, and zoomed through the heavy front door, slamming it behind them with a resounding thud.

Everyone on Linden Street agreed: The Dunwoodys might be an improvement over the McMartins, but they were still clearly insane.

The quiet, gangly girl was named Olive. Right now, she was eleven years old, but she would turn twelve in October. For her last birthday, her parents had given her a pile of books, a box of paints, and a fancy graphing calculator that Olive still hadn't used for anything except playing games. And she wasn't very good at the games, either.

The man with the forgotten push mower and the woman with the forgotten groceries were Olive's parents, Alec and Alice Dunwoody, two mathematicians who taught at a college nearby. Their hands were often smudged with ink. When they moved, chalk dust floated softly from their clothes. Unfortunately, the math gene had not quite reached Olive's twig on the family tree. The only time Olive ever earned an A on a math test, Mr. and Mrs. Dunwoody had taped the test smack in the center of the refrigerator door and then stood in front of it, holding hands, beaming at the paper as if it were a window into some magical, mathematical world.

Olive didn't know much about math. However, since moving to Linden Street, she had learned a few things about magic.

For instance, Olive knew that by looking through a pair of old spectacles the McMartins had left in the house, along with everything else they owned (their paintings, their dusty books, their three talking cats, their ancestors' gravestones embedded in the basement walls) a person could make Aldous's paintings come alive. A person could climb into these paintings and explore. A person—perhaps a quiet, gangly, lonely person—could even bring the portraits of Annabelle and Aldous McMartin to life and let them out into the real world, putting herself and everyone she cared about in terrible danger.

Although Olive had managed at long last to get *out* of danger again, she had also managed to break the spectacles. (If Olive had been half as good at math as she was at breaking things, her parents would have been very proud.)

Of course, Olive kept the things she had learned to herself. If her parents knew that she believed their house had been besieged by dead witches—witches who came out of paintings, no less—they would probably have taken her straight to the mental hospital. The neighbors up and down Linden Street already looked at Olive a bit strangely, as if she had some creepy, contagious rash that they didn't want to catch. They gave her tight little smiles, glancing out of the corners of their eyes at the big stone house all the while. Olive certainly wasn't going to confide in *them*.

There was another reason Olive didn't tell anybody about the cats or the paintings or the McMartins. She always put this reason second, even in her own head, but the truth was that her secrets would be a lot less *fun* if she shared them with anyone. Sure, a candy bar tasted good if you ate one half and let your dad have the other, but it was much, much nicer to eat the whole candy bar by yourself.

So Horatio, Leopold, and Harvey worked very hard to behave like normal cats when Mr. and Mrs. Dunwoody were around. Olive never mentioned the spectacles or climbing in and out of paintings. And every single day, she stood for a while in the upstairs hall, pressing her nose against the painting of Linden Street, thinking about Morton, the small, once-human boy who was stuck inside, and thinking about herself, still stuck out here.

As Horatio had once said, the painted version of Linden Street was as close to home as Morton could get. Without a family, a heartbeat, or a body that could grow up, Morton didn't belong in the real world anymore. But as someone who used to have all those things, he didn't quite belong in a painting, either. Olive was still hoping to find the place where he *did* belong, but in spite of all her thinking and nose-pressing, she hadn't found a way to get inside the paintings on her own—or a way to help Morton out for good.

And so, eventually, everybody in the big house on Linden Street settled down into a quiet routine, like a bunch of friendly but distant planets orbiting around each other.

Olive waited for something interesting to happen. She didn't know it, but the house was waiting for something too.

2

By the end of July, the weather had turned hot and muggy. Mr. and Mrs. Dunwoody spent most weekday afternoons in their offices at the college, where there was air-conditioning. They invited Olive to come along, but Olive didn't like her parents' office, where people talked in numbers instead of words, and where there was nothing to do but find patterns in the bumps on the ceiling.

On one of these long afternoons, Olive had the house to herself. Because it was made of stone and surrounded by a thick canopy of old trees, the house never quite got hot inside, but it felt humid and still and very quiet, like a bottle full of fog. The afternoon sun pushed blurry swathes of color through the stained-glass windows. Shadows spread beneath heavy antique armchairs. The picture frames on the walls glimmered faintly. Standing in the silent, stuffy living room, Olive looked at the painting of a couple at a sidewalk café in Paris and imagined wandering through narrow French streets, eating a croissant, tossing crumbs to the pigeons. That sounded like fun. Then she sighed, and, for the thousandth time, touched the spot where the spectacles had once hung around her neck.

She trailed up the carpeted staircase that led from the foyer to the upstairs hall. The painting of the little lake where Olive had found Annabelle McMartin's locket gleamed softly on the wall halfway up the flight. Annabelle had once tried to drown Olive in that same little lake, but today the water looked harmless, peaceful, even refreshing. Olive blew a puff of air through the wisps of hair that kept getting stuck to her forehead and imagined dabbling her toes in that cool water. Then she remembered the sensation of the lake swirling around her, black and oily, while her kicking feet brushed against cold, slimy things, and the waves closed over her head . . .

She hurried the rest of the way up the stairs.

In the upstairs hallway, Olive stopped at the painting of Linden Street. She had stood in this same spot so many times that the carpet had a little divot where her feet pressed it down. Inside the painting, a misty green hill rolled away toward an old-fashioned version of Linden Street, where the same wood and stone and brick houses occupied by Olive's neighbors stood in an unchanging twilight. Even without the spectacles, things that had once belonged in the real world—things that Aldous McMartin had hidden or trapped—could sometimes be seen moving inside of their paintings.

Squinting hard, Olive examined the row of houses. Perhaps she was just wishing, but she thought she could see a few small, pale figures bobbing and shifting in the distance. Maybe Morton was one of them. Olive pressed her nose to the canvas, and then jumped backward in surprise when the painting shifted with her touch. When the Dunwoodys first moved into the old stone house, all the paintings had been magically stuck to the walls. Now, with the McMartins out of the way, they could be nudged and moved just like ordinary paintings, and Olive hadn't quite gotten used to this. She straightened the painting of Linden Street. Then she sighed again and shuffled into her bedroom.

Horatio was asleep on Olive's vanity. His long body was balanced along the narrow shelf, and his gigantic feather duster of a tail wound delicately through Olive's collection of old pop bottles. Annabelle's locket, emptied of its portrait and its powers, was wrapped around the neck of one of Olive's favorite pop bottles: the bright green one covered with bumps that felt like Bubble Wrap. Once, the locket had been wrapped around *Olive's* neck, and she'd thought she would never get it off again. But now that the McMartins were gone, the locket was just one more magical thing that had faded into something normal.

"Horatio?" said Olive.

The cat didn't move.

"Horatio?" said Olive, more loudly.

"Mmmph," the cat grunted.

Olive wriggled her toes against the floorboards, steeling herself. "Will you please take me to visit Morton?" she asked, keeping her voice as un-whiny as she could. "It's been days and days since I've seen him."

Horatio didn't reply.

"I said, would you please take me to—"

"I heard you, Olive. Even though I was *asleep,* I heard you." Horatio turned his head very slightly, and Olive saw one green eye glaring at her from the reflection in the mirror. "Go ask someone else to take you."

Olive gave a giant sigh. Then she trudged out of the room, glancing up at the painting of Linden Street and hurrying past the bare spot at the head of the stairs where the painting of the moonlit forest used to hang, and which still felt a bit more menacing than a bare bit of wall had any right to. She thumped down the steps, along the high-ceilinged hall, and through the empty kitchen, all the way to the basement door.

Although Olive had gotten used to the basement, she hadn't grown especially fond of the place. It was always shadowy and dirty, and full of spiders, and even if she couldn't see them, she knew that the ancient gravestones were there, embedded in the chilly walls.

Olive opened the door and switched on the first light. Its weak glow revealed a rickety wooden staircase dwindling away into the darkness. "Leopold?" Olive called, venturing down the steps. "Are you there?"

At the foot of the staircase, she groped for the next lightbulb's hanging chain, but it seemed to have disappeared. Wasn't this where it should be, right at the bottom of the steps? She waved both hands through the air. The darkness of the basement seemed to thicken, the stone walls exhaling cool, damp breaths that tickled the back of Olive's sweaty neck. She was just about to give up, turn around, and bolt back up the stairs when her palm struck the chain. She pulled it so hard that the lightbulb rattled.

A pair of bright green eyes flickered in the corner. Even though she expected to see them, the sight still made her heart give a shuddery little jump. Then a gruff, familiar voice said, "At your service, miss."

Olive tiptoed across the gritty basement floor and into the shadows. The gigantic black cat was poised on the trapdoor just as he had been when Olive first met him, as rigid as a statue, his fur as dark and shiny as an oil spill. Long ago, Annabelle McMartin had hidden the urn of her grandfather's ashes under that trapdoor. Then, not so very long ago—and with Olive's unwilling help—Annabelle had taken the urn back out again.

Standing at the edge of the trapdoor, Olive could almost feel the wind of the painted forest where Aldous's ashes had whirled up, blotting out the sky, whispering across her skin like a million black insects as she and Morton had raced toward the safety of the picture frame—

She shook her arms, brushing both the memories and the imaginary insects away.

"What are you doing, Leopold?" she asked, crouching down beside the trapdoor and trying to force her heartbeat to return to normal.

"Standing guard," answered the cat, puffing out his chest. "The price of safety is eternal vigilance, you know."

"But there isn't anything down there anymore."

Leopold opened his mouth as though he might be about to argue. Then he shut it again. He cleared his throat, lengthily and elaborately, before speaking. "A soldier doesn't question his orders."

"But who *gave* the orders?" asked Olive.

There was a long pause. Leopold, standing at attention, stared straight ahead so hard that his eyes began to cross.

"Never mind," said Olive quickly, worried that Leopold might hurt himself if he thought any harder. "I just wondered if you would take me into the painting to visit Morton."

"Hmm," said the cat. "That would mean leaving my post, miss. It's against regulations."

"I see." Olive nodded. "Well, what if instead of leaving your post, we just stayed here, and maybe . . . went through the trapdoor?"

Leopold gave his head a violent shake. "Absolutely impassible, miss. I mean astutely imparsible. I mean NO."

Olive knelt down on the chilly stone floor and scratched Leopold between the ears. Slowly, his head began to tilt toward Olive's hand. "Come on," Olive wheedled as Leopold's eyelids slid down to half-mast. "You would be with me the whole time. I just want a peek. A little, teeny-tiny peek. Please?"

Leopold caught himself. "Simply impossible, miss," he announced, jerking back into his soldierly pose. "I am prepared to do a great deal for you, but I will not allow you to go underground. And I'm afraid I cannot go AWOL."

"Go A wall?"

"Absent Without Leave," Leopold enunciated, obviously pleased to have to explain. "If you'd like, at fifteen hundred hours we could engage in a game of

Clue here at my base of operations. As long as I get to be Colonel Mustard," he added.

"Fifteen hundred hours?" repeated Olive. "Noon is twelve, plus one is thirteen, plus two is . . ."

"Three o'clock," Leopold whispered helpfully.

"And we'd have to play down here?"

"I'm afraid I can't leave my station, miss. Not while you're home alone."

Olive glanced around at the stone walls pooling with darkness in the corners. A small carved skull in the stonework gazed back at her from the vicinity of the washing machine. "No offense, Leopold, but I don't like it down here."

"No offense taken," said Leopold. He appeared to think for a moment. "Where is Harvey?"

It was a good question. Olive hadn't seen Harvey all morning, and this was generally a bad sign. The last time Harvey hadn't been seen for two days, Olive and Horatio had finally found him in the garden shed, wearing a dented pirate's hat and helplessly tangled in an old hammock, which Harvey insisted was ship's rigging. "Captain Blackpaw will never surrender!" he had yowled as Olive extracted him.

Now Olive clumped up the basement stairs, feeling frustrated and a bit mopey, and looked around the empty kitchen. "Harvey?" she called. "Harvey?" But Harvey wasn't there, or in the dining room, or the parlor, or sleeping on the cool tile in the upstairs bathroom.

Olive walked along the hall into the pink bedroom, where the air smelled like dust and mothballs, and where the entrance to the attic was hidden by a painting of an ancient stone archway. It had taken Olive ages to find the attic's entrance, even with the spectacles. Without the spectacles, she couldn't get in at all. With a huff of frustration, she put her lips as close to the canvas as she could without actually touching it, and yelled, "Harvey!" at the top of her lungs. There was no answer.

Olive trailed back down the staircase and stepped out onto the front porch. The warm, dewy air felt almost stifling, like a stranger's breath on the back of her neck. She glanced around the overgrown lawn. The thick ferns swayed in their hanging baskets, releasing their spicy scent into the air. The old porch swing shifted lightly on its chains. Nothing else moved. Frowning, Olive turned back toward the door. And that was when she spotted it.

On the scuffed gray boards of the porch, the green print of a cat's paw stood out like a traffic light. Olive knelt down and touched the paw print. It was made of paint—paint that was still fresh enough to smear on her fingers. She stood up and took a careful look around. At the bottom of the porch steps, her box of birthday paints was spilled in a pile. The tube of green paint was open and oozing a trail that wound through the long grass toward the backyard.

Curiosity bumped the boredom and frustration right out of Olive's mind. As far as she knew, the cats never went far from the house. Even when Olive brought them outside, they zoomed back toward the doors like furry magnets. If Harvey had wandered away, there was no telling what sort of trouble he would find. The only thing that was certain was that he *would* find it.

"Harvey?" Olive called.

No one answered.

It was difficult to find traces of green paint on a green lawn. Olive had to get down on her hands and knees and squint, but here and there, she spotted a green splotch on a dandelion, or half of a paw print on a dry leaf.

The trail of clues led to the end of the Dunwoodys' backyard, where the ancient maple trees layered their thick shadows over the mossy ground. Still crawling, Olive noticed a streak of bright green on the leaves of the lilac hedge that separated the Dunwoodys' property from Mrs. Nivens's. Olive peered between the leaves, making sure that Mrs. Nivens's sunhat-topped figure was nowhere to be seen, and wriggled through the branches.

"Harvey?" she called, under her breath. But there was no cat to be seen on Mrs. Nivens's perfect lawn, or in her flowerbeds, or in the branches of her neatly pruned trees.

Olive skulked across Mrs. Nivens's yard, where tall shrubs and a fence divided the lawn from the alley. Mrs. Nivens, clipping coupons in her living room, noticed a pale blur moving through her hydrangeas, but reached the window too late to see anything but a telltale tremor from the borderline of Mrs. Dewey's birch trees next door.

Olive crouched in the knot of papery birch trunks, looking around for the next clue. If mystery books had taught her anything (and they had taught Olive much of what she knew), there was always another clue to find, if the detective knew how to look. And, as it happened, the next clue was hanging right in front of Olive's face.

A long green tail, with blotches of many-colored fur peeping through, twitched in the leaves above her. Olive looked up. Perched in the branches was the rest of a green-painted cat.

"Harvey!" Olive exclaimed. "What are you doing?"

The cat glanced over his shoulder. "Shh," he hissed. "Don't blow my cover. Call me by my code name: Agent 1-800."

Olive lowered her voice. "What's going on, Agent 1-800?"

"Climb up, and I'll give you a quick briefing."

Olive pulled herself onto the lowest branch of the birch tree. Harvey moved aside to give her room and left a few more streaks of green on the tree's white bark.

"It's going to take forever to get that paint out of your fur," Olive whispered.

"Camouflage was necessary," Harvey replied in an accent that was faintly British, turning his streaky green face toward Mrs. Dewey's backyard. "Sometimes a secret agent must do unpleasant things in the line of duty." He ran one paw across his nose, smearing away a drip of paint. "Here's the info. Top secret. Classified. For your ears only."

"Understood," whispered Olive.

"A foreign element has infiltrated the home territory."

Olive thought of the table of elements that hung in the science classroom at her last school. Were any of them foreign? She supposed a lot of them came from other countries. "What do you mean?" she asked. "Like Lithuanium?"

"Like *this*," said Harvey, pushing aside a leafy branch so that Olive could peek through.

Below them, in Mrs. Dewey's shady backyard, a boy sat at a wooden picnic table. Both the picnic table and the boy looked rather tired and dirty. The boy was smallish, thin, and long-limbed, with dark brown hair that curled and stuck up in various directions. He wore wire-frame glasses and a gray T-shirt with a picture of a dragon on the front of it. He was painting a model castle with a miniature brush, and frowning a little, the way people frown when they're trying to thread a needle.

"Who is that?" Olive asked.

"That's the foreign element. The infiltrator. The *spy*."

The boy put down the first paintbrush and picked up an even tinier one. He dabbed carefully at the edge of the castle. Olive noticed that both the boy and the picnic table were spattered with dots of paint, but the castle was immaculate.

"What makes you think he's a spy, Agent 1-800?" she whispered into the cat's ear.

"Just look at him!" hissed Harvey. "The devious smile. The shifty eyes."

Olive leaned forward, trying to get a better look at the boy. And, at that moment, the boy realized he was being watched. He stopped dabbing at the castle. Slowly he looked up into the green-gold leaves of the birch tree, where Olive and Harvey sat, staring straight back at him.

"Rutherford!" hooted a voice.

Mrs. Dewey's round body, looking extra snowman-like in a snug white sundress, came trotting quickly across the lawn.

"Rutherford Dewey," Mrs. Dewey huffed, "just look what you're doing to my picnic table! And to your shirt!" Mrs. Dewey tugged the tiny paintbrush out of the boy's hand. "What did I tell you about spreading newspapers on the table? Now go rinse your shirt before the paint sets in."

The boy took one last, silent look at the tree. His eyes met Olive's. For what seemed like a long time, they stared at each other, each trying not to be the one who blinked. Then Mrs. Dewey grabbed the boy by the shoulder and hustled him toward the house.

Harvey let out a breath. "That was close, Olive," he said. "Next time, you'd better paint yourself before going undercover."

HARVEY, STILL GREEN and forbidden to come inside until he wasn't, spent the night on the porch steps. The next morning he was nowhere to be found.

Olive knew he was probably hiding nearby, postponing a bath for as long as possible, so she lay on the back porch trying to read a Sherlock Holmes book while Horatio dozed on a windowsill and Leopold patrolled the basement. She would rather have been exploring than reading, but once again, both nongreen cats had made excuses when she asked them to take her Elsewhere.

She didn't like having to ask them in the first place. Olive was the type of girl who would rather climb a teetering stack of chairs up to a high shelf than ask for help, perhaps because she had a lot more practice at falling down than she did at talking to people. Back when she had the spectacles, she could go wherever she wanted, whenever she wanted, without having to ask anyone's permission. Now she had to beg three moody cats for the favor. It made her whole body itch just to think about it.

It was another humid, lazy day. Linden Street was soaked with sun, its green lawns sparkling and gardens blooming. Behind the big stone house, however, the yard was dim and murky. Towering trees cast a net of shadows over the jumbled garden. In one far corner, near the compost heap, a patch of bare dirt marked the spot where Olive had buried the painting of the forest, with a howling Annabelle McMartin still trapped inside. It looked like a fresh grave. And no matter where Olive moved to try to find a patch of light, the shadow of the house seemed to follow her. Once or twice, she nodded off in the sun and woke up in the humid shade, with her face stuck to the book's pages.

She was just peeling her cheek off of *A Study in Scarlet* for the third time when she noticed a flurry of movement across the backyard. She crawled to the edge of the porch. At the back of the lawn, deep in the overgrown dogwood shrubs, a branch rustled.

Olive left her book on the steps and tiptoed across the grass.

"What do you have to say for yourselves now?" a

voice hissed from the dogwoods—a voice with a faintly British accent. Olive crouched down next to the shrubs.

"So, you refuse to talk, do you?" she heard Harvey say. "Well, we have ways of encouraging you. Perhaps we will chip your lovely paint—like this!" There was a little *tink* sound of a claw hitting metal. "Still not talking? Oh, you're a stubborn bunch, aren't you? But we have a few more tricks up our sleeves—"

"Aha!" shouted Olive, thrusting the dogwood branches apart with both arms. "Found you!"

"Gah!" shouted Harvey, so startled that he toppled over backward.

"What on earth are you doing, Harvey?"

"*Agent 1-800!*" the cat spluttered, struggling back to his feet. His paint-splotched fur had dried so that it stuck up in some directions and was smooshed flat in others. Little leaves and twigs clung to it like Christmas ornaments. "I was interrogating these enemy spies, but they refuse to give up their secrets." Harvey turned back to his captives with a burning glare.

Olive followed Harvey's eyes. Among the dogwood twigs stood a row of little metal figurines. They were models of knights, some on horseback, others holding raised swords. The models had been carefully painted, right down to the teeniest details. Harvey was right about one thing: They weren't talking.

"Where did you get these?" Olive asked, although she already had a pretty good idea.

"They were captured on enemy territory," said Harvey. He inched closer to Olive, his eyes wide. "Who knows what dangerous secrets they are keeping?"

Olive looked down at the figurines. They stared back at her innocently.

"Excuse me," said a voice.

Now it was Olive's turn to topple over backward. Harvey leaped out of the dogwoods and caromed toward the branches of a nearby maple tree.

Olive looked up. Beside her stood the boy from Mrs. Dewey's backyard. He was slightly cleaner than yesterday, but he still looked as if he'd been hustled out of bed a few hours too early. His brown hair stuck up in confused, curly tufts. He was wearing a different T-shirt. This one had a dragon on it too.

"I think your cat took my models," said the boy in a rapid, slightly nasal voice.

"I guess . . . I mean . . . you mean these?" Olive scooped up the figurines and held them out to the boy between her fingertips, being careful not to actually touch him. "Sorry."

"I'm an expert on the Middle Ages," the boy blurted. "Well, on the Middle Ages in Western Europe, primarily Britain and France. I'm a semi-expert on dinosaurs. My favorite right now is the plesiosaur. I used

to like the brachiosaurus—that was the largest of the sauropods—but now I'm more interested in aquatic dinosaurs. Have you ever heard of the coelacanth?"

Those were the words the boy said. He said them so quickly, they sounded more like this to Olive: "Iusedto-likethebrakiosoristhatwasthelargestofthesoreopods-butnowI'mmoreinterestedinaquaticdinosaurshave-youeverheardofthesealocanth?"

"The seal what?" said Olive.

"Coelacanth," the boy repeated. He jiggled back and forth on his feet while he spoke. "A living fossil. A coelacanth was caught by a fisherman near South Africa in 1938, when everybody thought they'd been extinct for millions of years. I have a theory that there are lots of other surviving species of dinosaurs, still living deep in the ocean, and we just haven't found them yet."

"Okay," said Olive very slowly.

"What about you?" said the boy. "What are your interests?" Behind their smudgy lenses, his wide brown eyes blinked at Olive expectantly.

Olive thought fast. She liked to read scary stories while eating Tang straight from the can. She liked to collect bottles from kinds of pop no one had tasted in forty years. She liked to decorate smooth rocks with fingernail polish. But all of these things sounded strange, somehow, when she said them aloud. So, instead, because the boy was still staring straight down at her, she said, "My house used to be owned by witches."

Immediately, she couldn't believe she had said those words. Aloud. Out of all the words in the world. If the universe had had a rewind button, Olive would have definitely pushed it. In fact, she would really, really have liked to rewind past the point when the boy had said "excuse me" and she had fallen over onto her behind.

The boy straightened his smudgy glasses. "Interesting," he said. "What kind of witches?"

"What kind?"

"White witches, green witches, dark witches . . ."

"Dark," said Olive with certainty.

"How did you find out about them? Were there record books or journals? Did you have an expert occultist examine the house?"

"No . . ." said Olive. "They left all their stuff here."

The boy stopped jiggling. He looked hard at Olive, and his eyes were large and very dark brown. "Interesting," he said again, but more quietly. "Have you found their grimoire?"

"Grimoire?" Olive repeated.

"Their book of spells."

Olive blinked. "No."

"You should look for it," said the boy. "Every witch has one. It might provide some very important information."

"Maybe," said Olive, feeling a bit angry that she hadn't thought of this before.

Meanwhile, the voice in her brain was shouting, *OF COURSE!* If she knew the McMartins' spells, maybe she could find a new way into Elsewhere! Maybe she could even make her own magic spectacles. Maybe there would be some hint about how to help Morton. Olive's heart began to pound.

The boy held up a knight figurine, turning it in the patchy sunlight. "This one seems to be chipped," he said. "I'd better go repair it." Abruptly, he turned and headed toward the lilac hedge. Then he stopped and looked back at Olive. "My name is Rutherford," he said.

"Like the president?" Olive asked. Olive had memorized all the presidents when she was six, after her parents had bought her a placemat with the presidents' names and pictures printed on it. Rutherford B. Hayes (number 19) had a bristly beard, and he was right next to Ulysses S. Grant (number 18), who had a slightly less bristly beard.

"No. Like Ernest Rutherford. The father of nuclear physics. He won the Nobel Prize in 1908. My parents are scientists. They're in Sweden, doing research."

Something in Olive's mind flashed with recognition. "My parents are mathematicians," she said. And before she could stop herself, she smiled at the boy. It was a crooked, slow, grimace-y sort of smile, but it was a smile nonetheless. "My name is Olive."

The boy smiled back. "I know," he said. Then he pushed through the lilacs and disappeared.

"TRAITOR!" shrieked a voice from the maple tree. Harvey's greenish head popped through the leaves. "Traitor! Turncoat! Benedict Arnold!!"

Olive stood up and brushed off the seat of her shorts. "Harvey—"

"AGENT 1-800!!" the cat yowled. He stormed along the branch above Olive's head. "How could you betray us to the enemy like that? How could you turn your back on your own countrymen?!"

"Harvey—I mean, Agent 1-800—come down. We can talk about this, but not out here. What if someone hears you?"

"What if someone hears *me*?" Harvey's eyes boggled. "What if someone hears *you*? You could be court-martialed! Exiled! Imprisoned for life!"

"For giving model knights back to the boy you stole them from?"

"Back to the master *spy*, you mean." Harvey hunkered down on the branch and stared at Olive intently. "Listen to me. *Do not trust him*. Don't believe anything he tells you. And don't trust that woman he is staying with, either."

"Mrs. Dewey?"

"She is not what she seems," the cat whispered. "Neither of them is."

"Harvey, this is crazy. Come down right now and take your bath."

Harvey stared down at Olive for a moment. Then he bolted toward the trunk and clambered up into the higher branches.

Olive rolled her eyes and turned back toward the house. Her book still lay open on the porch, but the breeze had moved its pages around, and she had completely lost her place. She didn't feel like reading Sherlock Holmes right now anyway.

She felt like reading something else.

THE LIBRARY WAS the biggest, dustiest room in the old stone house. It had a huge, tile-framed fireplace that looked as though it hadn't been used in years, a painting of dancing girls in a meadow (who Olive knew for a fact were not as friendly as they looked), creaky rolling ladders reaching up to the ceilings, and battered velvet furniture with leaky stuffing trailing across the cushions like thick gray cobwebs. The library walls were lined with bookshelves that ran from the floor all the way up to the high ceilings, and every inch of the shelves was crammed with books. Olive guessed that it would take a person a hundred years to read all of them. Of course, that was just about how long Annabelle McMartin had lived.

Most of the books were very old. They were bound

with cloth or leather, and the gold-painted words on their spines were fading. Olive loved to read, but she didn't love to read these sorts of books. They had titles like *A Thoroughly Thorough and Exhaustive Exploration of the Fascinating Lives of Snails,* and *The Woeful Tale of a Maiden Who Went About without Her Tippet.* Once Olive had taken down a book titled *Wild Birds and How to Dress Them,* thinking it might have some good suggestions for catching birds and making tiny costumes for them to wear, but the rest of the title, which couldn't fit on the cover and had to be printed on the front page, was *A Treatise on the Most Modern Methods of Plucking, Stuffing, and Basting Game Birds, Containing Sixty Hand-colored Engravings of the Most Delightful Dishes Together with Invaluable Hints for the Home Cook.* Olive had put the book back.

Now she stood in the middle of the library and felt the dust tickling her nose. If the McMartins had left behind a book of spells—a *grimoire,* the boy had called it—then it made sense that it would be here, with all the other books. The memory of Rutherford Dewey's eyes lighting up when she'd blurted those words—*my house used to be owned by witches*—made Olive's whole body itch with embarrassment. *Why* had she said it? Why had she told him anything at all? Olive grabbed two fistfuls of her hair and yanked. *Stupid,* she told herself. *Stupid, stupid, stupid.*

She glanced around the library. One important, secret book could easily blend in with thousands of others. A whole book full of the McMartins' plans and spells could be right here, hiding in plain sight!

The problem was where to begin.

Olive knew that the books weren't arranged in any particular order. They weren't alphabetized or sorted by subject, like in school libraries. Books about plants nobody had ever heard of were next to books about politicians nobody had ever heard of, and with the print rubbing off of the covers, a person would have to open up most of the books to be sure of what was inside.

Olive dragged the rolling ladder along the wall to the room's right-hand corner. She climbed to its highest step, took a firm grip on the top shelf, and pulled down the very first book. A skin of dust smudged off on her fingers as she turned the book over. *Lineage of the Russian Tsars*, said the cover. Olive opened the book. A man wearing a hat that looked like a hairy cake stared back at her. There were no spells to be found here.

The next book, *Tales to Terrify Impudent Children*, was a bit more interesting, but it wasn't what Olive was looking for. Flipping through the pages of each book and sneezing every now and then, Olive made her way slowly to the end of the first shelf. She was thumbing through a copy of *Truly Marvelous Advancements in the Manufacture of Canadian String* when a voice from below nearly startled her off of the ladder.

"What are you up to?" demanded Horatio as Olive wobbled and clutched the shelf for safety.

"I'm just . . . looking," said Olive.

Horatio settled himself on the Oriental rug. "Yes, I suppose that's what one usually does with a pair of eyes and a book," he said. "Are you *looking* for anything in particular?"

"Sort of," she said slowly. "Horatio, did the McMartins have a . . . a grimoire? You know, some kind of book of spells?"

Horatio looked up at Olive, his sharp green eyes scanning hers. "Why do you want to know that?"

"Just out of curiosity."

Horatio blinked at her. "Olive, are you trying to kill me?"

"What?"

"You know: 'Curiosity killed the cat.'"

A little smile tugged at the corner of Olive's mouth. "Horatio, are you making a joke?"

Horatio gave a shrug that was almost bashful, and examined his toes.

"So," Olive wheedled, looking through her lowered eyelashes at the gigantic orange cat, "*is* there a grimoire somewhere?"

Horatio sighed. He flopped over onto the rug, stretching his whole body into a furry orange parenthesis and then slowly spreading each individual paw. Bones realigned, he rolled into sphinx position and looked up at Olive. "There *was* a spellbook, yes," he said, "although it was an incomplete record of the things the McMartins could do. Let's just say that there are some types of magic that can't be learned from a book. In any case, I haven't seen the spellbook in more than seventy years. Aldous hid it, or Annabelle destroyed it, and either way, I doubt very much that you'll find it."

Naturally, this made Olive want to find it even more.

"But you cats were their assistants," she argued. "Shouldn't you know where something as important as their spellbook went?"

"Precisely. We *were* their assistants. Things stopped being warm and friendly between the McMartins and the three of us long before the spellbook disappeared. Aldous could still force us to obey, but he didn't trust us anymore." Horatio turned away, padding a sunny patch of the rug with his paws. "And now, I would suggest that you listen to a wise old saying, and let sleeping cats lie."

"That's *dogs*," corrected Olive.

Horatio, already in napping position, ignored her.

Holding tightly to the ladder with one hand, Olive rolled along the wall to the next set of shelves and took down the first two books: *A Tremendous Hullabaloo* and *Whatever Shall We Do About Hortense?* Olive slumped on the step. Densely packed shelves surrounded her, covering the library walls from floor to ceiling. Even if the titles on the antique spines had been clear, the McMartins were certainly clever enough to hide a book of spells inside some misleading cover. Olive had done this herself sometimes. A paperback mystery fit very easily inside her math textbook.

It had taken her about fifteen minutes to look through the books on one shelf. There were four sets of shelves along each short wall, and six shelves along the longer walls, spaced between two tall windows, the fireplace, and the painting of girls frolicking in a meadow. Each set of shelves had nine shelves within it. If she added and then multiplied the total number of shelves by the number of minutes she spent on one shelf . . . The numbers ran around inside Olive's head and smashed into each other like a bunch of blind football players. It would take her *a very long time*.

She pulled down the next book, inhaled a puff of dust, and sneezed until she could see spots.

"That's one good thing about you, Olive," murmured Horatio from the rug far below. "You're not a quitter."

Olive rubbed her itchy nose and got back to work.

The sun was casting peach-colored trails through the library windows when Mr. Dunwoody strolled in, whistling "Inchworm" cheerily to himself. "Inchworm" was Mr. and Mrs. Dunwoody's special song. They had danced to it at their wedding, and in fact were probably dancing to it in the photo that sat on Mr. Dunwoody's desk, in which a younger Alec and Alice beamed at each other in the middle of a tiny dance floor, romantic light reflecting off of the lenses of their large round glasses. These days, Mrs. Dunwoody wore contacts.

Mr. Dunwoody settled himself in the chair at his desk. Horatio made a beeline out of the room.

"I don't think that cat likes me," said Mr. Dunwoody.

"He doesn't *dislike* you," said Olive, perched like a bookish spider in one high corner. "He's just sort of . . . reserved."

Mr. Dunwoody looked up, startled. "Oh, hello, Olive. I didn't know you were in here."

"Then who were you talking to?"

Mr. Dunwoody stared thoughtfully up at the ceiling. "That's a valid question."

Olive blew a bit of dust off of her fingers. "Dad, about how many books do you think are in this room?"

"A rough estimate?" Mr. Dunwoody scanned the walls. "Twenty shelving units, nine shelves on each, and an average of forty-five books per shelf? Eight thousand one hundred books, give or take."

Olive ran her fingertip across a row of battered spines as if she were playing a mute piano. "What if a person spent thirty seconds looking at each book, just flipping through the pages? How long would it take to look at all of them?"

Mr. Dunwoody tilted happily back in his chair. "Thirty seconds per book equals 243,000 seconds, equivalent to 4,050 minutes, or to 67.5 hours."

"That's what I thought," said Olive. "A very long time."

"A 'long time' is relative," said Mr. Dunwoody. "Time itself is relative."

Olive, who had been told this sort of thing as frequently as other children are told to brush their teeth, nodded obediently. "Well, do you think it's almost time for dinner, here and now, in real-world time?"

Mr. Dunwoody sniffed the air. "Judging by the scent coming from the kitchen, I would say yes."

"Good." Olive climbed stiffly down the ladder, feeling sore in more ways than one. She was probably no closer to finding the book she was looking for, and even worse, the memory of her own voice blurting out "My house used to be owned by witches!"—*to a complete stranger*—made her flush with fury at herself every time she relived it. Why on earth had she told that boy her biggest secret?

"Dad," said Olive as she and her father walked down the hall toward the lovely smell of lasagna, "if you told somebody a secret, and you weren't sure you could trust that person to keep it a secret, what would you do?"

"Hmm," said Mr. Dunwoody. "That's tricky. People are so unpredictable. However, I would say your safest course of action would be to balance the equation."

"What do you mean?" asked Olive, envisioning two numbers hopping onto a teeter-totter.

"If you know something about this other person that he or she wishes to keep secret, then he or she is less likely to tell *your* secret, and risk you telling his."

"Isn't that like blackmail?" asked Olive, pulling out her chair at the table.

"I would say it's more like Newton's third law," said Mr. Dunwoody, carefully straightening his placemat so that it was parallel to the edge of the table. "Every action has an equal and opposite reaction."

"I already straightened the placemats, dear," said Mrs. Dunwoody, approaching the table with the lasagna pan.

"Yes, darling. But you know how I feel about parallel lines . . ."

Mrs. Dunwoody smiled. "That their perfection gives them their identity."

"And that's also just how I feel about you," said Mr. Dunwoody, kissing the back of his wife's hand.

Olive sighed and laid her head down on her dinner plate.

OLIVE COULD HARDLY sleep that night. Little half-dreams of whirling stacks of books and messages written backward on mirrors kept knocking around inside her brain. Sometimes the messages said things like, *The spellbook is in the bloobquepoo,* or some other nonsense that was no help at all. Other times, the message said, *My house used to be owned by witches!* and as Olive watched, the message reflected from one mirror to another and another and another, unfurling into a huge web of repeated words. The web was tangling around her. She was stuck in it, pinned in place and unable to escape. Only the book could help her. It would keep her safe. It would save Morton. She had to find it, before anyone else did. She thrashed and kicked, her heart revving up to panic mode—*The BOOK,* went her heartbeat, echoing inside of her own head. *The BOOK. The BOOK. The BOOK. The BOOK.*

Something let out a loud hiss.

Olive jerked awake and found that she had been kicking wildly at the sheets. Horatio, who liked to sleep at the foot of the bed, was glaring up at her from the floor.

"I'm sorry, Horatio," Olive whispered. "I was having a nightmare."

"I see," huffed the cat. "Well, don't worry about me. Although it *is* harder to land on your feet when you're *asleep*."

"Sorry," Olive whispered again.

Horatio hopped back onto the mattress, giving Olive's feet a wide berth.

"I did something stupid today," said Olive, picking up Hershel, her worn brown bear, and squeezing him tightly against her collarbone.

"Imagine that," the cat murmured.

"And now I can't sleep, because I just keep thinking and thinking about it."

"Sounds very productive," said the cat, settling back into the blankets.

"There's this boy living with Mrs. Dewey," Olive went on as Horatio let out an exasperated sigh, "and he's the one who asked me about the spellbook. But he only asked me about the spellbook because . . ." Olive's voice dwindled to a mumble. ". . . Because I told him about the McMartins."

Horatio turned sharply. "What, exactly, did you tell him?"

"I just told him that witches used to live here. I didn't even say their names." Olive rubbed Hershel's head with her chin, which was usually very comforting. Tonight, it wasn't. "I don't know why I said anything at all."

For a moment, Horatio gazed at the window. Moonlight reflected in his eyes, making them glow like delicate fires. "This boy is living with *Mrs. Dewey,* you say?"

"Yes. His name is Rutherford Dewey."

"Then I wouldn't worry too much about it," said Horatio, nuzzling into the covers.

"But I *am* worried!" said Olive. "I keep thinking and thinking about it." She nudged Horatio gently with her foot. "Horatio, I'm not going to get back to sleep. Could we go visit Morton? Just for a little while? Please?"

Horatio sidled away from Olive's nudging toes.

"Please?"

The cat gave Olive a hard look. "*If* I take you, will you promise to let me spend the rest of the night without getting booted out of bed?"

"Yes. I'll even sleep sideways."

"Fine." Horatio leaped lightly to the floorboards

and trotted through the door. Olive hurried after him, but she turned back for just a moment to tuck Hershel under the covers.

Squares of moonlight through distant windows gave the upstairs hall its only light. Horatio moved sound-lessly over the thick carpet. Olive tiptoed behind him, listening to the house creak and shift, taking up as little space as she could in the darkness.

They stopped in front of the painting of Linden Street. "Hold on," Horatio commanded. Olive grasped his tail. The moment her fingers were buried in the cat's fur, Olive saw the painting come to life. Soft breezes rippled the misty grass. Far in the distance, lights from the houses twinkled and flickered. Horatio hopped over the frame's bottom edge, dragging Olive's arm after him. With the familiar sensation of sliding through warm Jell-O, Olive pushed her head through the frame, and then her shoulders, and then her whole body was toppling forward, over the bottom of the frame, into the painting.

She landed in the dewy grass on the other side. The frame floated in the air above her. Horatio, who nat-urally landed on his feet, was already heading up the soft green hill toward the street, where a few lamps glowed like welcoming beacons. Olive got up and hur-ried after him.

It was always evening in Morton's world. A faint,

misty twilight swaddled the painted version of Linden Street, never turning darker or brighter. On this street, no one ever had to go to bed, or come inside for dinner, or get their pajamas on. In fact, since most of the people in this painting had been lured straight out of their beds and into Aldous McMartin's canvas, they were already wearing their pajamas anyway.

The first time Olive had visited this painting, the street was eerily still, and faces had peered at her distrustfully through the tiny windows of locked doors. Now the faces peered at her and smiled. Through many of the closed curtains came the soft glow of candles or lamplight. A few people even sat on their porches in the silvery mist, rocking gently on porch swings. One old man in a nightcap raised his hand in a wave. Olive waved back.

Horatio trotted ahead of her, up the pavement, past the empty spot where the big stone house would have been if Aldous McMartin had painted it, toward the tall grayish house just beyond.

"I'm going to get you!" someone shouted.

Olive jumped. Horatio bristled.

The sound of laughter trailed around the corner of the tall gray house. Instinctively, Olive crouched down in the dewy grass, trying not to be seen. A moment later, a small boy in a long white nightshirt raced around the house's side, panting and chuckling, reaching out as if he were trying to catch something that dangled in the air just in front of his face. His nearly white hair stood up in tufts, and his face looked like a smiling moon.

Giving the empty air a wild swipe, the boy tripped on the hem of his nightshirt and sprawled on the grass, laughing. "All right," he declared, getting back to his feet. The grass where he'd landed got back up too. "You win this time."

Olive blinked hard. She scanned the entire lawn, but she still couldn't see anyone but the boy in the white nightshirt. Who was he talking to?

"That means I'm still It," the boy announced to the empty yard as he trotted up to the front porch railing. "I'll count to one hundred. Ready, set, GO!" He put his face down on his arms and began to count.

Olive and Horatio exchanged a dubious glance. With a last slow look around the yard, Olive tiptoed toward the porch steps.

"Pssst . . . Morton!"

"Twenty-eight— What?" The boy in the nightshirt looked up, and a smile broke across his round, pale face. "Olive!" he exclaimed. The smile disappeared. "You made me lose count."

"Sorry. Are you playing hide-and-seek?"

"Yeah." Morton beamed, hopping down the steps. "I'm It."

Olive glanced around again. The nearest person she could see was an old woman in a rocking chair on the porch next door, several yards away. She certainly didn't seem to be hiding. "But . . . Morton . . . who are you playing with?"

"My friends," said Morton, with a silent *obviously* at the end.

"I don't see anybody here," said Olive.

"Of course you don't," said Morton. "They're invisible."

"Invisible?" Olive repeated. "Do you mean they're . . . um . . . imaginary?"

Morton gave a one-shouldered shrug. He grabbed the bottom post of the porch rail and swung back and forth. "Maybe. But they still play with me. They play with me more than *some* people. Some people who you really *can* see." He cast a pointed look in Olive's direction.

"Morton, you know the spectacles got broken. I can't come in here whenever I want to anymore. I have to get one of the cats to bring me." Olive glanced over her shoulder at the fuzzy orange bulk of Horatio, who was currently sculpting his whiskers.

Morton started swinging in such wide arcs that Olive had to step out of the way. "My *real* friends come and play with me whenever I want them to, because they know I don't have—" Morton stopped in mid-swing, glancing up at the dark windows of his big, empty house. Olive could almost hear the words *a family* hanging in the air, but Morton didn't finish the sentence. Instead, he spun around and pointed across the yard. "Ronald is hiding right over there, under that porch. Charlotte Harris is the one behind those bushes, and Elmer Gorley always wears plaid pajamas. You can come out, guys!" he yelled toward the street.

They waited, Morton smiling, Olive frowning, as Morton's invisible friends approached.

"This is Olive," Morton told the empty yard. "I've told you about her. . . . Yep, she's the one who helped me get rid of the Old Man."

"Helped *you?*" interrupted Olive.

Morton ignored her. "No, she doesn't know how," he went on, answering a question Olive hadn't heard. "She still hasn't figured it out. So we're all stuck here until she does. Besides," he said, dropping his voice to a whisper and bending toward someone's invisible ear, "I don't think she's really trying. Most of the time, she's probably just doing *girl* stuff. Playing with dolls. Fixing her hair."

"I don't even have any dolls!" Olive protested.

Morton giggled, as though one of his invisible friends had said something funny. He looked at Olive, hiding his smile behind one cupped hand. "Yeah, she does, doesn't she?"

"Well," said Olive loudly, putting her clenched fists on her hips, "I came here *in the middle of the night* just to see you. I could be in my bed right now, all warm and comfortable. But I guess I didn't need to. With all your new friends, I guess I don't need to worry about you at all anymore."

"I don't think you really do worry about me," said Morton in a low voice.

"Of course I do!" said Olive, throwing her arms up. "I think about how to help you all the time."

"But you're not *here* all the time." Morton studied a spot on the misty ground. "And I am. All the time."

"You know I can't stay here, Morton. If I wait too long, I'll get stuck here too."

This seemed to trouble Morton for a moment. Olive could see his chin working as his face moved from sad to angry and finally back to uncaring. "I know," he said at last, sharply, tossing his head so that the white tufts quivered. "That's why I have these other friends." He glanced over his shoulder. "They'll stay with me until—until something else happens."

Olive shuffled her feet. The painted grass hurried to straighten itself wherever she smushed it flat. "I really am trying, Morton."

Morton nodded, but he didn't meet her eyes. "Well, I'm going to start counting to one hundred again."

"Oh," said Olive, surprised. She took a step backward. Morton had been crabby and even rude in the past, but he had never been too busy for her before. "I guess . . ." she said, and then didn't know what to say next. She turned away from Morton's house. Across the lawn, two bright green eyes glimmered, watching her.

"Wait!" She spun back toward Morton, who looked up from his counting once again. She shook the hurt feelings off of her face and put on what she hoped was a blank, businesslike expression. "I really just came to ask you something. When you lived next door to the McMartins, did you ever see Aldous or Annabelle with a book of spells?"

Morton gave a tiny jump at the mention of the Old Man's name, and out of habit, glanced up at the sky. Its soft blue-violet hue didn't change.

"I mean," said Olive, "with any book that looked really old or strange or special?" Morton was already shaking his head, but Olive went on. "Maybe it had symbols on the cover, or weird-colored ink . . ."

"No," said Morton. "I don't think so."

"Okay," said Olive. "One more thing. Did you ever know anybody with the last name Dewey?"

"Of course he didn't know the Deweys," snapped Horatio, who had appeared suddenly next to Olive's shin. "The Deweys didn't move in until nearly fifty years after Aldous McMartin died." The cat gave a sigh. "Olive, I'm leaving. If you would prefer to stay here and turn into paint, be my guest." He flounced toward the sidewalk. "In fact, it would be nice to have the whole bed to myself."

"I'm coming," said Olive, scurrying after the cat. She turned back to wave at Morton, but he was already counting to one hundred, with his face hidden in his arms.

Olive followed Horatio down the street and onto the soft green slope of the field. Ahead of them, the picture frame glinted softly in the misty air. She glanced over her shoulder at the row of houses. Morton himself had disappeared, presumably chasing an invisible friend, but his big gray house still loomed in its place, its emptiness echoing with questions.

"Horatio . . ." Olive began, rather slowly. ". . . Did Morton have parents? I mean, he must have had parents. Right?"

"Well, he didn't sprout from an acorn," said Horatio. When Olive just blinked down at him, the cat heaved a sigh. "*Yes,* Olive. He had parents."

"What happened to them?" Olive's mind clicked through the years, trying to remember Aldous's age, and Annabelle's age, and how old Morton was when Aldous trapped him in the painting, and then to subtract all of those numbers from the year it was now, while trotting down a foggy hillside at the same time.

Even when she'd gotten to the end of the equation, she felt sure 1822 wasn't the answer to her question. "They'd be really, really old now, wouldn't they?"

Horatio's eyebrows went up. "Yes," he drawled. "One hundred and twenty is rather old for human beings."

Olive slowed. Mist swirled around her ankles, filling in the holes left by her footsteps. "So, did they— did they *die*?"

Horatio paused beside her. He glanced away, toward the hanging picture frame, as he answered. "I can't say for certain what happened to them."

Olive sidled around the fluffy orange cat so that she could see his face. Horatio didn't meet her eyes. In fact, he looked distinctly uncomfortable. *Suspiciously* uncomfortable.

"Did Aldous do something to them?" Olive demanded, with growing certainty. "Did *you* do something to them?"

Horatio's eyes hardened. "Well, Morton's parents *did* raise a bit of a ruckus in the neighborhood when their little boy vanished from his bed in the middle of the night," he said dryly. "You know how parents can be. So overprotective. Aldous needed them out of the way before they drew too much attention to the McMartin family."

Olive crouched down in front of the cat, blocking

his path. She stared into his green eyes until at last they looked back at her, and the cool, sarcastic set of Horatio's face began to melt.

"I don't know exactly what happened to them," Horatio said, after a long, quiet moment. "I believe they were—disposed of. By *him*."

"Disposed of?" Olive pictured Morton's parents whirling down the drain of a slimy garbage disposal. It wasn't a pleasant image. She studied Horatio's face again. He gazed back at her with an unusually misty look in his bright green eyes.

Olive let out a deep breath. She looked back at the twinkling lights already dimming in the distance. "If he doesn't have a family, it's nice that Morton has some friends here," she said. "Even if they're invisible."

Horatio gave her a keen look. "It's nice that you think it's nice."

"What do you mean by that?"

"I mean, some people don't like to share their friends. Especially people who only have one."

"I don't only have *one*," argued Olive. "I have more than one." She looked down at her bare toes. "I have you."

A tiny smile uncurled on Horatio's face. "I see," the cat mumbled, patting his whiskers. "Very well." He glanced up at Olive, the smile back under control. "But I'm never going to play hide-and-seek with you."

"Fine," said Olive.

Together they climbed through the picture frame.

Still, Olive couldn't help thinking about Morton and his *other* friends while she climbed back into bed and settled Hershel beside her on the pillow. Even in her dreams, she saw Morton's face. She saw him standing before his huge, empty house, with no mother or father waiting inside. She watched him running through the misty fields, chasing a friend who wasn't there, while she was stuck on the outside of his world, with no way in.

She had to find that spellbook so that she could help Morton. She had to find some answers. And she had to find them *soon*.

6

FOR BEST EFFECT, *apply the leeches to the inside of the throat using a leech glass or a large swan's quill,* Olive read, and immediately started coughing. She shoved *The Healthful Effects of Bloodletting* back into its spot high on the third set of shelves, which was as far as she had gotten in a whole morning of searching the library. Across the room, the dancing girls in the painting of the meadow seemed to be smirking at her. Olive guessed that, if she could have seen them, the faces of Morton's invisible friends would have worn the very same expression.

Morton's words from the night before still stung and itched in her mind like a mosquito bite. *She still hasn't figured it out.* Much as Olive hated to admit it, Morton was right. She hadn't formed a plan, the spellbook was nowhere to be found, and Olive's head was getting cluttered with things she didn't want or need to know. "What on earth is a leech glass, anyway?" she muttered to herself.

"A leech glass was a long glass tube, sort of like a test tube," said a very fast voice from below. "A rolled piece of paper could be used for the same purpose. Leeches have been used in medicine for thousands of years, including during medieval times, which is why I know all about them. In fact, the word *leech* comes from the Old English word for *physician*."

Olive froze, balanced on the top of the ladder. At the far end of the room, standing in a cluster by the library door, were Mrs. Dunwoody, Mrs. Dewey, and Rutherford Dewey. They were all looking up at Olive. It was Rutherford who had been speaking, of course. Beside him, Mrs. Dewey gave a halfhearted smile. Mrs. Dunwoody looked a bit stunned.

"Olive, you've met Rutherford, haven't you?" said Mrs. Dunwoody. Compared to Rutherford, Mrs. Dunwoody seemed to be speaking in slow motion. Olive nodded, biting her tongue. "He's going to spend the afternoon here with you."

Inside of Olive, something started screaming. She bit her tongue even harder.

"I have an appointment in the city," explained Mrs. Dewey, tugging on a pink jacket that fit around her body like a balloon fits around its ball of air. "Mrs. Nivens is away for the afternoon, and besides, I thought it would be much nicer for Rutherford to spend the day with someone his own age for a change." She gave her grandson a significant look. "Rutherford could do with some *normal* young friends."

Olive chewed on the inside of her cheek.

"Well," said Mrs. Dunwoody cheerily, "he's more than welcome. Take as much time as you need, Mrs. Dewey." And the two women bustled out of the library, leaving Rutherford and Olive alone.

Rutherford strode toward the center of the room. Mrs. Dewey had obviously tried to make him look presentable. His curly brown hair had been doused with water and combed flat to his skull. He was wearing a pair of severely ironed pants and a T-shirt emblazoned with a big crest of a lion fighting a serpent. He was also wearing a huge, heavy-looking pair of metal gloves.

Olive examined Rutherford between her eyelashes. She couldn't look him in the eyes. He knew her secret. A boy like Rutherford Dewey certainly wouldn't have forgotten what she'd said. And now she had to spend the whole afternoon with him—a boy, a *stranger,* someone "her own age," who would definitely notice and remember every single odd, awkward thing she did or said.

"Have you found it?" asked Rutherford.

"Found what?" said Olive, who could barely make her mouth work, let alone her brain.

"The grimoire. I'm sure this room is the most natural place to look." He stopped at the foot of the ladder, staring up at Olive through his smudgy lenses.

For a second, Olive fought with herself. Was it too late to lock the secret up again? It probably was. Besides, trying to talk to a boy she barely knew was hard enough. Without any time to prepare, her brain didn't feel capable of talking and lying at the same time. "I haven't found it yet," she finally said, but the words got stuck, and she had to clear her throat and start over. "I checked all of these shelves, but I have the rest of the room to do."

"I could help you," said Rutherford, jiggling in his loafers. "I'm a very fast reader. I can read about seventy pages in an hour, depending on the size of the font, of course."

Olive wanted to scream *NO!* and shove him out of the library. Actually, *she* didn't want to shove him; that would mean touching him. Ew. What she really wanted was a giant, invisible hand to close around Rutherford and drag him out of the room, down the street, and all the way to Norway or Finland or wherever he'd said his parents were.

But that didn't happen.

"You don't have to help," she mumbled.

"I would be happy to. I'll have to remove my gauntlets, though." He tugged on the strap fastened around one wrist. "Normally, I wouldn't, but it's hard to turn pages with them on."

"I'll bet," said Olive.

Rutherford held up his left hand to give Olive a closer look, still speaking a mile a minute. "These are replicas, of course, but they're still very authentic. I got them at a renaissance festival, and the craftsman modeled them after German gauntlets from the fourteenth century. The rondel is deceptive, because it looks like a mere decoration, but it was actually for blocking maneuvers."

Olive nodded very slowly.

Rutherford dropped the gauntlets gently onto the rug. "Now, just because I'm laying down my gauntlets, it *doesn't* mean that I'm challenging you to a duel."

"Oh," said Olive. "Good."

They spent the next hour searching the shelves in near silence. Olive stayed at the top of the ladder, and Rutherford paged through the books closer to the floor, occasionally mumbling "Interesting," or "Is that so?" to himself.

While Rutherford seemed to be skimming through the books at lightning speed, Olive couldn't focus. She felt too nervous to even breathe. She didn't want

Rutherford here, that was for sure. Furthermore, she had the sense that the *house* didn't want him here. Someone or something was watching them, she was certain—just as certain as she'd been all those many moments when she'd ducked just in time to feel a spit-wad or snowball go whizzing past her ear. As time ticked by, the library seemed to get darker and quieter, until each turning page sounded like a giant, rattling sheet of tin. The walls seemed to be leaning in around them. They wanted to push Rutherford out too.

Olive hoped they *wouldn't* find the spellbook. She didn't want to share any more secrets with this boy. Fortunately, she felt increasingly certain that the book wasn't in this room at all.

"Are you going to be in sixth grade or seventh grade of junior high this year?" Rutherford asked abruptly, without looking up.

The words *sixth grade* and *junior high* always made Olive's stomach squirm and clench, as if they were grubs she had swallowed whole. "Sixth," she managed to answer.

"So am I," said Rutherford. "We'll be going to the same school. I'll be staying at my grandmother's house for at least a year while my parents conclude their research."

There was a soft rustle from the big potted fern by

the fireplace. Olive stared at the plant for a moment, but it didn't move again.

"I've already attended seven different schools throughout the U.S., Europe, and Canada," Rutherford went on, "but my parents thought it would be better if I stayed here this time."

The fern gave a soft hiss. Rutherford didn't seem to notice.

"Wow," said Olive softly. "I've only been to four different schools." Bad memories darted through her, nibbling at her stomach like a horde of tiny, needle-toothed fish: days of no one to eat lunch with, days of being picked last for teams, days of spending recess sitting near the playground fence, pulling up shoots of grass just to look like she had something to do. She took a breath. "Do you mind it? Changing schools over and over, I mean?"

Rutherford shrugged. "It can be hard to adjust," he said. "But I just tell myself that everything is temporary. Wherever I am, I won't be there for long."

Olive nodded, but somehow this thought made her sad.

They both turned back to their books, and for a moment, the library was quiet, even the fern.

Olive coughed uncomfortably. Rutherford, cross-legged on the floor, went on thumbing through a big green book. Olive coughed again, and this time the cough went on and on, until her eyes started to water and Rutherford turned to look up at her.

"I—um. I . . . I mean," Olive said, and coughed again. "That thing I told you. About this house?"

"Yes?" said Rutherford.

"Don't—don't tell anyone, okay?"

Rutherford gazed at her very seriously. He nodded. "I give you my word. I'll even take an oath, if you want me to. I could sign something, or I could lay my hand on a holy book—"

"No, that's . . . You don't have to do that," said Olive. "Just keep it a secret."

"Certainly. I vow not to tell a soul," said Rutherford. Then he stood up and gave Olive a low, courtly bow before plopping back down with the green book.

"Interesting," he murmured a moment later.

"What's interesting?" asked Olive, who was feeling *almost* (but not quite) friendly toward Rutherford, now that he'd promised to keep her secret.

"This book claims that Captain Kidd was the only pirate known to have buried his treasure." Rutherford gazed up at the ceiling. "I wonder if your witches might have buried their treasures, like the grimoire, somewhere. But I suppose, being witches instead of pirates, they would have used a disappearing spell instead. Have you seen any evidence of disappearing spells?"

Olive wondered how a person could see evidence of

something that had disappeared. She shook her head. "No. They didn't—"

She stopped midsentence. Because the McMartins *had* made things disappear.

They had made people vanish forever. They had made men and women and children disappear just as completely as if they *had* been buried. They had hidden things where no one else could find them—no one but Olive. Maybe everything she was searching for had been hanging right in front of her face . . .

Rutherford didn't seem to notice that Olive had trailed off. He was still sitting on the floor, skimming through a dusty book (and Olive was still staring off into space, thinking, with her mouth hanging open) when Mrs. Dewey came to take Rutherford home.

"I'll help you search again tomorrow, if you want," Rutherford offered, getting up and pushing a heavy blue volume back onto the shelf.

"That's okay," said Olive, as loudly and quickly as she could. "I—I'll let you know if I need help. Thank you."

"All right. You know how to summon me." Rutherford stopped at the door where Mrs. Dewey was waiting, fastened his gauntlets, and gave Olive another long bow in farewell.

"Help look for what?" Olive heard Mrs. Dewey ask as she and her grandson headed into the hall.

"Oh, we were doing some research on the history of dinosaurs in this area. What particular species lived here, when they became extinct . . ."

The voices faded away, and Olive breathed a sigh of relief. He was gone. The whole room seemed to brighten, as though the air itself grew lighter. Rutherford had kept her secret—so far, anyway. And now it was *their* secret. Maybe that would be enough to balance the equation.

Olive glanced up at the trails of afternoon sunlight slanting through the windows. A beam struck the frame around the painting of the dancing girls, and suddenly the whole frame flared and glittered as though it had been electrified, its golden sparkle lighting the way forward. The idea that had formed in Olive's mind began to flare and sparkle too. The spellbook's hiding place was so obvious! Why hadn't she thought of it before?

Just then, something greenish, damp, and feline belly-crawled out of the potted fern. "So, the spy is gone at last," it gasped, struggling across the floor.

"Harvey!" Olive scrambled down the ladder. "I thought it was you."

"I can't fight it any longer," the cat wheezed, rolling his eyes toward the ceiling like a bad Shakespearean actor. "I only regret . . . that I have but one life . . . to give to my country."

Olive crouched beside him, putting one tentative hand on his fur, which was stiff with green paint and coated with leaves. "Are you hurt?"

"No," Harvey whispered. "But the time has come . . . for a BATH." And then he collapsed dramatically in the middle of the rug.

THAT NIGHT, HORATIO curled up in his usual
spot at the foot of the bed. Harvey, still smelling
strongly of cat shampoo, headed down the hallway to
the pink bedroom, to guard the entrance to the attic.
Mr. and Mrs. Dunwoody both peeped in to wish Olive
sweet dreams. Then the hallway lights clicked off and
the house settled down into sleepy darkness.

With her head on the pillow and Hershel tucked
under her chin, Olive listened to the low creaks and
groans of the old stone house, and to the twigs tapping
softly on the window glass. All of this was familiar
now. Inside her own bedroom, Olive felt almost safe,
even in the darkest part of the night. But she sensed
that while she and her parents went to sleep, the house
never did. It was always awake. Watching. Olive wasn't

sure if this was a good or a bad thing—if the house was watching out *for* her, or if it was watching *her*.

She lay very still, waiting, repeating the words to catchy songs over and over in her head to stay awake. After she had gone through "I'm Henery the Eighth, I Am," about twenty-five times (she lost count somewhere around thirteen), she sat up very slowly and blinked out into the darkness over Hershel's fuzzy head. She had a plan: a plan to make Morton *her* friend again, and if her hunch was correct, to find the spellbook too.

The room was silent. Horatio was a motionless lump of fur. Even the distant white glow of the streetlamps had faded above the sleeping street.

Olive slid her legs to the edge of the mattress, careful not to bump Horatio. The big orange cat didn't stir. The floor felt cold against the soles of her feet, but, as usual, none of her six pairs of slippers were waiting by the bed where they belonged. She slunk across the room and slipped out the door into the hall.

The floorboards creaked as Olive tiptoed past the paintings of the bowl of strange fruit and of the church on the craggy hill. She hurried by the dark, open doorways of the bathroom and the guest rooms, trying not to imagine anyone jumping out at her, any voices whispering her name from the shadows inside. But it was hard not to.

By the time she reached the front of the house, she was nearly running. She darted through the doorway into the pink room.

Harvey was asleep on a chair before the painting of the old stone archway that was the entrance to the attic. His head hung limply over the edge of the seat.

As gently as she could, Olive tapped the cat's front paw.

Harvey sat bolt upright. "The royal fleet awaits your command, Majesty!" he declared.

"Shh!" Olive hissed. "Harvey, I need your help. I know where something I've been looking for might be hidden." She stared into the cat's wide green eyes. "Will you help me?"

"I'm afraid you have mistaken me for someone else, Your Majesty," said Harvey, straightening himself on the cushioned seat before taking a regal bow. "Perhaps you do not recognize me after my long months spent at sea. It is I, Raleigh, Sir Walter Raleigh. And I am at your service."

"Okay, Sir . . . who did you say?"

"Sir Walter Raleigh. Explorer, writer, soldier, and all-around Renaissance man."

"Okay, Sir Walter Raleigh," said Olive. "But we have to be very, very quiet. No one else can know about this mission. You're the only one I can trust."

The cat gave a delighted nod.

"All right," Olive breathed. "Now, we're going to

go out into the hallway, into the painting of Linden Street, and we're going to find Morton."

"Ah yes, the good Sir Pillowcase!" said Harvey with growing excitement. "We will navigate the straits and join our comrade!"

"Sure," whispered Olive. "You navigate. I'll be right behind you."

Sweeping an imaginary cape over his shoulders, Harvey leaped from the chair and flounced toward the door. Olive tiptoed after him.

She followed Harvey's fuzzy silhouette back down the hallway. In front of the painting, he offered her his tail, and together they clambered through the frame into the misty field below Linden Street.

They found Morton sitting on the lawn of the house next door to his own, which in Olive's world belonged to Mrs. Dewey. He was yanking up a row of white tulips and flinging them into the air, where they spun end over end like floppy batons. Then they zoomed back toward the ground, bulbs first, and planted themselves neatly in their waiting holes.

"Morton, what are you doing?" asked Olive as she and Harvey stopped in front of him.

Morton gave her a look that said this question didn't really deserve an answer. He pulled up the next tulip.

"Where are your friends?"

Morton shrugged. "Somewhere. Maybe they're at

home. With their families." He threw the tulip into the air. It flipped over twice and dove back toward the ground like a lawn dart.

Olive wanted to say, "Are their families invisible too?" but looking down at Morton's face, she decided not to. Instead, she crouched down on the dewy grass. "Hey, Morton," she began. "Do you remember that book I asked you about?"

Morton pulled up another tulip and didn't answer.

"I think if I could find that book, I might learn how to help you get back home."

Morton looked at her out of the corner of one eye. "*Real* home?"

"*Real* home," Olive repeated. "If the McMartins had a book of magic spells, they probably kept it in a magical place. I think that book is hidden in a painting somewhere inside this house."

Morton's round face turned skeptical. "Maybe."

"So . . ." said Olive, trying to sound as though she really didn't care, "will you help me look for it?"

"Oh," said Morton, trying to sound as though he really didn't care either, ". . . I suppose I could."

"Excellent!" boomed Harvey. "An agreement has been reached between Good Queen Bess and the noble Sir Pillowcase. Now, onward, to explore the colonies!" And he charged off down the misty street, with Olive and Morton struggling to keep up.

Once they had all wriggled through the frame, they stood uncertainly in the hallway, glancing around at the dark, open doorways. "Where should we start?" Morton whispered at last.

Olive closed her eyes. She thought about the book. She imagined its cover, black or brown or red or green. She imagined the feeling of its pages. Maybe they would be heavy and soft, almost like cloth, or maybe they would be fine and delicate and nearly transparent, crinkling one over another like sheaves of tissue paper. And, very faintly, very gradually, something in the house began to guide her. It leaked out of the walls and rippled up through the floorboards into the soles of Olive's bare feet. She could feel it turning her in the right direction, like the spinning arrow in a board game.

"I don't think it's downstairs," she whispered back. "Let's start up here."

They threaded their way along the hall, Harvey trying to stay in the lead, even though he didn't know where they were going, and Olive and Morton walking behind, tiptoeing on each other's shadows.

They began their search in the guest bathroom, which had only one small painting. With Olive holding on to Harvey's tail, and Morton holding on to Olive, they tugged each other through the frame. The woman in the painting, who was perpetually posing with one toe in the water of an old-fashioned bathtub, let out a little shriek when a splotchy cat and two pajama-clad children dropped through the frame onto her slippery tile floor. She plunked down into the water, towel and all.

"Pardon us, good lady," said Harvey grandly, "but we must explore your bathroom, for the glory of England."

"What!?" bubbled the woman.

Olive crouched down to look under the bathtub while Morton checked the corners. The room inside the painting was quite small and bare, and in just a few seconds, the three explorers were clambering back out of the frame, leaving the dripping lady huffing angrily behind them.

"No book there," whispered Olive. "Let's check the blue room."

The blue bedroom was dark and grim, full of things like hat racks and shoe stands and dressers with rows of heavy, creaking drawers. On one wall there hung a painting of a ballroom where people in evening clothes danced to the music of an orchestra. But when Harvey, Olive, and Morton came stumbling through the frame, the people stopped dancing. A few last tweets and blats came from the orchestra as one by one the musicians lost their places and gaped at the intruders.

"Be at your ease," said Harvey with a generous wave of his paw. "No doubt you are awestruck by the presence of the great Sir Walter Raleigh and the most splendid Queen Elizabeth." He gestured to Olive, who tugged uncomfortably at her penguin pajamas. Harvey glanced over his shoulder at Olive and Morton, and said out of the corner of his mouth, "These ruffians know not how to bow to their queen. Shall we have them all beheaded, Your Majesty?"

Olive shook her head vehemently. "Um—actually," she began, while all the painted eyes of the crowd swiveled toward her, "excuse us, but have any of you seen a book in this room?"

The crowd started to murmur.

"I saw one!" shouted one man from the corner, pointing, but the book he'd seen turned out to be only the big book of sheet music on top of the piano.

"I saw one too!" shouted another man, but he turned out to be talking about the same book as the first.

"Okay," said Olive loudly as more and more people joined in, proclaiming that they too had seen the book of sheet music on top of the piano, "has anyone seen a *different* book? *Not* the one on top of the piano?"

There were some confused mumblings, but no one else spoke up.

"All right, then," said Olive. "Thank you for your help."

"Jiminy," whispered Morton as they landed one by one on the blue bedroom's carpet. "Those people weren't very bright."

"You speak the truth, Sir Pillowcase," Harvey agreed.

"Well, they're just paintings," said Olive. "They've never been out of that one room. I'm sure they don't have to do much heavy thinking."

Morton looked down at his toes and didn't answer.

"I mean," Olive hurried on, "they're not like *you,* or like the other people Aldous trapped in the paintings, who used to be real, but who aren't—I mean, you haven't always been just—I mean—"

But Morton was already stalking across the room toward the polished wooden door of the closet.

"Morton . . ." Olive pleaded.

Morton ignored her. He stepped into the closet and slammed the door behind him.

Olive sucked in a breath through her teeth. Had her parents heard? She and Harvey exchanged glances.

"I shall ensure that no adversarial vessels have entered the straits, Your Majesty," the cat whispered, dashing out into the hall.

"Morton," said Olive to the closed closet door. "Come out of there."

There was no answer. Olive pulled on the knob, but the door wouldn't budge. Morton was obviously holding it tight on the other side. "Come *on,* Morton," she said. "We're wasting time."

The closet was silent for a moment. It seemed to be thinking. Then a muffled voice from inside said, "Why can't I just stay out here? If the Old Man is gone, how come we all can't just come out again?"

"Morton, you're not *alive*." Olive paused. "Anymore." The closet didn't argue, so Olive went on. "People would notice that you don't get any older, and your skin looks funny, and you don't eat anything. And bright light burns you. You wouldn't be safe out here."

"I could live in the closet," said Morton stubbornly. "Or everybody from the painting could just live in this house with you."

Olive tried to imagine this. "I don't think that would work," she said at last. "My parents would tell all the scientists from the college about you, and they'd all want to do tests on you and dissect you and genetically clone-splice you or something."

The closet got very quiet.

Olive leaned her head against the wooden door. "Morton . . ." she began, as gently as she could. "I—"

But his voice interrupted her. "There's a painting in here."

Olive frowned. "Why would anyone hang a painting in a closet?"

"It isn't hanging. It's leaning. I can feel it. Look."

The closet door swung open. Morton stepped out of the darkness, shoving aside a few musty wool coats and pointing to the closet's back corner. There, lit by a beam of watery moonlight, a picture frame glinted around a painted canvas.

On their knees, Olive and Morton dragged the painting out into the blue room for a better look. Inside the heavy frame was a picture of a ruined castle, its stones crumbling beneath a night sky.

"Do you think it's one of *his* paintings?" Morton whispered.

"Well, I know how we can find out for sure," Olive whispered back as Harvey swaggered into the bedroom to announce that the coast was clear.

A moment later, the three of them were climbing through the picture frame, into a cool, damp, moss-scented night. So it *was* one of Aldous's paintings—one that Olive had never explored before. While they teetered across the mossy rocks that led down to the moat, she wondered how long it had been waiting in the closet, and who had put it there in the first place, in a spot where no one would ever get to look at it.

The trio paused at the drawbridge. Harvey gazed at the crumbling stone walls before them and shook his head sadly. "The years have not been kind to Windsor Castle."

"I don't think it's supposed to be—" said Olive.

But Harvey was already marching over the drawbridge, with Morton at his heels. Olive wobbled across the slippery planks behind them.

Inside the castle was a wide, stone-paved courtyard. If the courtyard had ever had a roof, it wasn't there anymore. Above the edges of the crumbling walls hung a dark sky spotted by a few changeless silver stars.

"Ah, what glorious memories Windsor Castle holds, even in its ruins!" said Harvey, bounding away across the paving stones. "What pageantry! What duels! What executions!"

As Harvey leaped up the steps to the parapet, reminiscing happily to himself, Olive and Morton searched the courtyard's chilly corners. There was no sign of an important book anywhere. A big, empty, roofless room in a big, empty, crumbling castle seemed like an awfully unlikely place to leave an important book anyway.

"It's not here. I'm sure of it," said Olive with a sigh as a flagstone she'd shoved aside wiggled itself back into place. "Sir Walter Raleigh! We're ready to go!"

As Olive and Morton passed through the arch leading to the drawbridge, Olive thought she heard something clatter in the distance behind them—something that sounded like a pebble kicked across the flagstones. A second later, she heard the soft rattle of the pebble rolling back to its original spot.

"Harvey? Is that you?" she called.

Harvey's green eyes blinked up from the darkness near her shin. "No, Your Majesty. Do you not recognize Sir Walter Raleigh, your most loyal knight?"

"I meant, did you make that noise?"

"What noise, Majesty?"

They all listened. There was no sound—nothing but the soft swish of the water in the moat rippling against its banks.

"I hear nothing, Your Majesty," said Harvey.

"Me neither," said Morton. *"Your Majesty."*

Olive narrowed her eyes at Morton. "Thanks, *Sir Pillowcase.* Let's go look in the next room."

With Harvey leading the way and Morton and Olive hurrying behind, they crossed over the drawbridge to the mossy bank. Olive took a last look back at the castle, standing silent and dark under the night sky. Then, together, they climbed out of the painting, shoving it carefully back into the closet and closing the door.

The trio slipped along the silent hallway, where traces of moonlight turned the walls to silver, and headed into the lavender room. This room had once been Olive's favorite. It had seemed sweet-smelling and delicate and pretty—just like Annabelle. Now Annabelle's empty portrait hung like a menacing reminder above the chest of drawers. Although none of the guest bedrooms were used by the Dunwoodys, the lavender room felt especially cold and deserted, as though sunlight never reached it at all. Harvey leaped onto the chest of drawers, Olive held his tail, Morton held her foot, and they all crawled through the frame and landed, one by one, on the pillowy couch inside the painting.

"This is where Annabelle McMartin's portrait was painted, back when she was young," Olive explained, wondering why she felt compelled to whisper. "It's the downstairs parlor of this house. A long, long time ago."

Hesitantly, Olive climbed off of the couch and stepped toward the tea table. Everything stood at the ready: the cups and saucers, the dish of sugar cubes piled as high as ever. Annabelle's full teacup sat just where she had left it. Olive touched the delicate porcelain. It was still hot. With a sudden shiver, Olive glanced around the room. It seemed that Annabelle would appear at any moment with her soft brown hair, her string of pearls, her gentle, too-sweet voice. Olive could almost feel the chilly touch of Annabelle's fingers closing around her hand. She turned back toward Morton.

Morton was making one slow revolution, like a wind-up ballerina in a jewelry box. "I've been here," he whispered. "Not the painting. The *real* here." He wandered away to the right.

Olive skirted around the tea table, where Harvey was practicing fencing positions with a butter knife, and started looking under the furniture. Nothing. Next, she examined the shelves, but they held only delicate curios, little vases and seashells, and frou-frou souvenirs. Just to see what would happen, she checked the doors. They had been painted shut, but not in the way that things are usually painted shut, when a little bit of paint dribbles into a gap and makes things stick together. These doors had been *painted shut*. They didn't move or rattle their hinges when she pushed them. The doorknob didn't even turn in her hand. With a discouraged sigh, Olive turned back toward the room.

Morton was standing beside the fireplace. At first Olive thought he might have fallen asleep on his feet, he was standing so still—but of course Morton didn't have to sleep. His back was to her, and he was huddled over something that he held in both hands so that Olive couldn't see what he was looking at until she was peeping right over his shoulder.

It was a photograph: a small black-and-white photograph in a silver frame. It had obviously been part of the row of photographs lined up on the mantelpiece. Olive looked at the other photos in the row. With a tiny shudder, she recognized the photograph of Aldous McMartin that she had found in a dresser drawer in the lavender room, just outside of this very painting. Next to Aldous's portrait was a photo of a pretty but sour-faced little girl sitting between two rather dim-witted-looking grown-ups: Annabelle with her parents, Olive was sure. This was followed by several photographs of people Olive didn't recognize.

She glanced back down at the picture in Morton's hands. It was another family portrait, probably taken in the 1910s or 1920s. The men wore suspenders; the women had square, ribbon-trimmed collars. Unlike in the other pictures, everyone in this photo was smiling. Two beaming parents were gathered with a teenaged girl and a little boy. The mother's eyes were big and gentle and turned down at the corners with her smile. The father's face was round and friendly. The teenaged girl had a face that was angular and smooth, and her smile was a bit stiff, as though it had been stored in a refrigerator until it set. She reminded Olive of someone. But it was her brother who caught Olive's eyes and held them. He was a little boy with a round, pale face. A little boy with tufty, whitish hair. A little boy who, for once, wasn't wearing a long white nightshirt.

"Hey, that's you!" she exclaimed.

Morton didn't answer.

"Is that your family?"

Morton nodded.

"Wow," Olive breathed. They were both quiet for a minute, studying the faces caught in fading shades of gray. "It must have been taken not too long before—I mean, you look almost exactly the same. Except in different clothes."

Morton just stared at the picture.

Olive edged around him, trying to get a look at his face. "Do you know what happened to them, Morton? To the rest of your family?"

Morton shook his head, not meeting Olive's eyes.

"What about their names? Do you remember their names?"

"Mama and Papa," Morton whispered.

"I mean their *real* names," Olive pushed. "What other people called them. If you can remember, maybe—maybe I can find out what happened."

Morton's frown twisted and wriggled as he thought. One by one, unhappy lines appeared in his face, pulling his eyebrows into a frown, tugging his mouth downward, wrinkling up the corners of his eyes. The lines deepened until his whole face seemed to crumple, like a plant wither-ing in fast motion. He hung his head.

"I want to go home," he said into his sternum.

"I know you do," said Olive. "That's why I need to find this book. If I find the book, and we find out what happened to your family, then we can—"

"No," said Morton, still speaking directly to his chest. "I just mean, back to my house."

"Oh," said Olive. "Okay." She backed away, trying not to show her disappointment.

"Can I take this with me?" Morton held up the pho-tograph, although he kept staring directly at the carpet.

"Sure," said Olive. "Of course. Maybe—maybe it will help you remember."

It was a quieter, slower group that trailed back down the hallway to the painting of Linden Street.

"Do you want to look with me again tomorrow?" whispered Olive as Morton took hold of Harvey's tail. Morton shrugged and didn't meet her eyes.

Olive watched the two of them disappear through the picture frame. Then she slumped into her bed-room and climbed between the covers. Her dreams that night were full of books that fluttered toward her, like big friendly birds, before slipping through her fin-gers and soaring away.

8

OLIVE WOKE LATE the next morning with the urge to dive back into Elsewhere burning inside her.

Something else was burning too. She could smell it. For a moment, as she lay in the foggy place between sleeping and waking, Olive was certain that the house itself was burning—that it had lulled her into a deep sleep and left her to smother in the smoke. She sat up in bed, glancing around at her bedroom walls. But there was no fire. There wasn't even any smoke. There was only an unpleasant burning smell . . . and it seemed to be coming from downstairs.

Olive followed her nose down to the kitchen, where Mr. and Mrs. Dunwoody were clanking and clattering through the drawers and cupboards. Four pots were boiling away on the crusty burners of the old black stove, creating the burning smell and making the kitchen even hotter and stickier than it would have been otherwise.

"Aren't you two going to your office this morning?" Olive asked grumpily, through a mouthful of toast. If her parents were around, the cats tended to hide, which meant all her plans for exploration would be squashed.

"Not today," said Mr. Dunwoody, who was testing the burners on the old stove to see which boiled water the fastest, carefully measuring the amount and starting temperature of the water. "Would you like to help me double-check the cooling rate of these pots?"

"Or you could be my Archimedes," said Mrs. Dunwoody, who was sorting the contents of the drawers according to weight and density, gesturing invitingly toward a bucket full of water.

Olive shook her head.

After breakfast, Olive sat on the back porch, scowling. She had brought a green Popsicle outside with her, but she'd already sucked out all the juice. All that was left now was a water-flavored icicle in a bag, and the bag kept cutting the inside of her cheeks.

She needed that spellbook. She felt sure that she'd been close to it last night, that it was somewhere upstairs . . . But what if she was only imagining this? Olive's imagination had the tendency to kidnap her and take her to dangerous places. What if the book wasn't even in the house? Or—worst of all—what if it had never existed in the first place?

No. She squashed the thought down into a hard little lump. She had the lurking, lingering feeling that she *had* seen the book somewhere. But *where*?

Olive stood up and wandered toward the back of the yard. She tilted the Popsicle bag in her hand, letting a trail of droplets fall onto the strange plants in the garden, where they sparkled on purple velvety petals and spiny stems and leaves that looked like pointed fingernails. Very carefully, because you never knew what was going to sting or make you itch in this garden, she pulled up one little pink flower and held it to her nose. It smelled like a swimming pool.

A warm, wimpy breeze floated across the yard, carrying with it the sound of someone humming in a rather tuneless fashion. Olive followed the sound. It led her toward the lilac hedge that separated the Dunwoodys' backyard from Mrs. Nivens's. Through a fence of thick green leaves, Olive could see flashes of a broad-brimmed sunhat, a yellow dress, an apron, and prim little shoes with curved, two-inch heels. *Who gardens in high heels?* Olive wondered to herself.

And suddenly, Mrs. Nivens's smooth, yellowish face was staring right back into hers. "Well, hello, Olive dear," Mrs. Nivens said, bending down to peer through the leaves. "I thought I heard you over there."

Olive jerked backward, smacking her head on a branch. She could feel her face progressing quickly from red to fuchsia. "Hello, Mrs. Nivens," she mumbled.

"You look awfully warm, Olive," said Mrs. Nivens. "Would you care for a glass of lemonade? I just made a pitcher. It's waiting right over here."

Making conversation with Mrs. Nivens over a glass of lemonade sounded about as pleasant as juggling tarantulas. But if Olive said no, Mrs. Nivens would think she was an even stranger, ruder little girl than she did already. So Olive stumbled through the lilac bushes into Mrs. Nivens's perfectly manicured yard and followed her to a little table with a ruffled umbrella that stood in the shade near the house. Mrs. Nivens poured Olive a glass of lemonade from a pitcher beaded with condensation. She didn't take one for herself.

Olive sipped her lemonade, feeling hot and sticky and itchy in places she couldn't scratch in public—certainly not in front of Mrs. Nivens. Mrs. Nivens, on the other hand, appeared to be as cool as ever, as if she had been carved out of a cold stick of butter. The smooth, chilly planes of Mrs. Nivens's body didn't seem to want to move. Or maybe they *couldn't* move. Maybe if Mrs. Nivens laughed or jumped or even looked surprised, she would shatter into a thousand pats of butter. Olive imagined Mrs. Nivens falling apart into a heap of small foil-wrapped rectangles. She had to bite the inside of her cheek to keep from smiling.

Today, in spite of the late summer heat, Mrs. Nivens was wearing a dress with long sleeves, and her legs— what little of them the dress's full skirt left exposed— appeared to be covered in panty hose. The thought of wearing panty hose in this heat made Olive itch even more.

They sat for a moment in silence. Mrs. Nivens adjusted the brim of her white straw sunhat.

"How is the lemonade?" Mrs. Nivens asked at last.

Personally, Olive thought it could have used about twice as much sugar and a lot less lemon, but she wasn't about to say so. "It's good. Thank you, Mrs. Nivens."

"Are you getting all settled into your new house?" Olive could feel Mrs. Nivens's eyes on her face, even through the curtain of her hair. "It's such a big place— there must be so much cleaning and organizing to do, so much old junk to clean out."

"It *is* big," said Olive. "But we haven't been getting rid of anything." She thought of the painting buried in the backyard and of what was stuck inside of it. "Not really."

"Hmm," said Mrs. Nivens. "I would think you'd want to remove some of the clutter. Have a yard sale, perhaps."

Olive took another tiny sip of lemonade. "Um, Mrs. Nivens . . ." she began, ". . . you lived next door to Ms. McMartin for a long time, didn't you? I mean—a long time before we moved in?"

"Yes," said Mrs. Nivens stiffly. "Yes, I did."

"I was wondering," said Olive, choosing each word very carefully, but trying to sound very cool and casual at the same time, "did you ever see anybody . . . *take* things out of the house, after Ms. McMartin died?"

Mrs. Nivens let out a short, breathy laugh through her nose. "Nobody could have gotten into that house," she said, tugging off her gardening gloves. "Even the ambulance staff barely made it through in one piece. *Those cats,*" Mrs. Nivens emphasized, her eyebrows rising just the teeniest bit. "They wouldn't let anyone through the door. And of course, soon the house was all locked up—and many of the valuables were stowed safely away, I'm sure. Annabelle was a very cautious person when it came to family heirlooms. Even though she had no family to leave those things *to* . . ." Mrs. Nivens trailed off with a skeptical little shrug. "I'm sure whatever was in there before is still in there now."

Olive let out a breath. *See?* she told herself. She'd felt quite sure that the spellbook was in there somewhere, just waiting to be found. Beneath the table, her feet began to tap impatiently.

"Why do you ask?" Mrs. Nivens's eyes were honed on her again.

"I—I was just wondering," Olive said, thinking fast. "There's a whole set of encyclopedias in the library, but the one for letter C is missing, and I was wondering where it went, because I wanted to look up . . . *carburetors*."

If Mrs. Nivens thought Olive's answer was suspicious, she didn't let on.

Olive gulped the rest of her lemonade and plunked the empty glass down on the table. "Well, I should probably get back home and help with lunch."

Mrs. Nivens stood and reached out to pick up Olive's empty glass. For a moment her ungloved hand passed through a beam of sunlight, and Olive, glancing down, saw that there was something funny about Mrs. Nivens's skin. She barely had time to wonder what it was before Mrs. Nivens had jerked her hand sharply back into the shade. Her eyes pierced into Olive's like two icicles.

"Good-bye, Olive," said Mrs. Nivens, in a tone that made Olive hop up and back away. "Good luck finding—whatever it is you're looking for."

Olive was already on the other side of the lilac hedge by the time Mrs. Nivens's words sunk in. *Whatever it is . . . ?* Maybe Mrs. Nivens hadn't believed the story about carbuncles. Or carburetors. Or whatever it was Olive had said. There was something strange about Mrs. Nivens, that was for sure—something even stranger than gardening in high heels.

The many windows of the old stone house stared down at Olive as she crossed the shady, overgrown lawn. She stared back. She was so busy staring that she didn't even notice the rumpled, mussy-haired boy in front of her until she'd nearly bumped into him.

"Hello," said Rutherford calmly as Olive let out a startled squeak.

"What are you doing in my backyard?" she demanded, backing away from him until she was stopped by the lilac bushes. She and Rutherford were almost exactly the same height, so Rutherford's eyes, which were watching her intently from behind his dirty glasses, were very hard to escape.

"I was looking for you, naturally," Rutherford answered. "My school schedule just came in the mail, and I thought we could compare and see if we'll be having any classes together."

"It came already?" Olive cast a dismayed glance at the paper in Rutherford's long, paint-speckled fingers. "But school is weeks away!"

"I'll have American history, Spanish, general math, art, and physical science during the first semester," Rutherford recited. "I'm a bit disappointed that it has to be physical science instead of geology or biology; even botany would be more useful to my possible future career, but I suppose that they don't allow those kinds of choices until high school . . ." he rattled on, jiggling from foot to foot.

As horrible as the thought of school was, it couldn't quite push the other thoughts out of Olive's mind. Her eyes drifted back to the windows of the big stone house, flicking from room to room: the steamy kitchen window, the stained glass of the dining room, the gauzy curtains of her own bedroom, the little round porthole of the attic. Somewhere, behind one of those watching windows, was the book that she was looking for.

"Have you found it yet?" Rutherford asked suddenly.

Olive jumped. For a second, she was sure Rutherford had been reading her mind—but maybe he'd only been reading her face. "Found what?" she asked warily.

"The grimoire," said Rutherford, jiggling with increasing excitement. "Have you finished searching the library?"

Olive hesitated. Something that didn't make sense— something she'd been too distracted by the promise of the spellbook to notice—rushed to the forefront of her mind, like a roadside construction worker waving a PROCEED WITH CAUTION! sign.

"Why are you so interested?" she asked slowly. "And how did you know about *grimoires* in the first place?"

Rutherford blinked back at her. "What do you mean?"

"I mean, how did you know that I should look for a book of spells? You said, 'Every witch has one.' How did you know that?"

For the first time since Olive had met him, Rutherford seemed to be searching for the right words. He stopped jiggling. His eyes drifted away from Olive's, toward the rustling lilac leaves behind her. "Well," he said, speaking much more slowly, so that his words came out only slightly faster than most people's ". . . The practice of witchcraft was apparently quite common in the Middle Ages. Stories of magic and sorcery, like Merlin and Morgan le Fay, and . . ." He trailed off, his skinny fingers turning the class schedule around and around. "Later, when writing became more widespread, witches were known to keep books of spells, but most of them would never let you—I mean, let anyone else—" Rutherford broke off again. When he began the next sentence, his voice had resumed its usual pace. "*Grimoire* is a French word; it comes from *grammaire*, which is French for *grammar,* so the word *grimoire* really implies a set of rules for language." His eyes flicked back to Olive's. Behind their smudged lenses, they looked wide and slightly alarmed, but more than anything else, they looked *hopeful*. "Have you found it?" he asked.

Olive looked back at him for a long moment. "No," she said at last. "I've been looking. But I haven't found it."

Rutherford nodded. "If you do find it, I would really like to see it. Even just as a historical artifact, it would be fascinating . . ."

Olive shuffled her feet in the long grass. "*If* I find it," she said noncommittally, looking away from him again.

"Well, I'd better be going," said Rutherford after a brief pause. "The silver paint on my model of Henry Tudor, Earl of Richmond, should be dry by now. I've got to add the details."

And with that, Rutherford whirled around and hurried along the side of the house toward the street. His whole body seemed to be leaning forward, as though his head was trying to move even faster than his legs could go. Olive wondered if he might topple headfirst over his own feet, but he made it safely to the sidewalk before striding out of sight.

She turned back to the dark windows of the old stone house. The book was inside the house somewhere. And only the house knew where it was. If the spellbook was bait, then Olive was the fish, and the house was slowly reeling her in.

9

"STOP PULLING," WHINED Morton as Olive tugged him toward the painting that led to the attic's entrance.

"I have to pull you or you won't get through," Olive argued. "Now hurry up."

"I can hurry without you pulling," Morton muttered.

They were in the pink bedroom, very late at night, where the scent of mothballs and ancient potpourri floated through the damp midnight air. Through the lace curtains, the dim light from the streetlamps filtered like white mist, and if she squinted, Olive could just make out the stern faces of two towering stone soldiers on either side of the massive arch in the painting that led up to the attic.

This painting was different from Aldous's other works. It didn't take you Elsewhere—it was not a little world that you could climb into. Stepping through the frame, you found yourself not in an ancient city at all, but in the dark entryway to the house's attic—the attic where Aldous had created all of his paintings a very, very long time ago.

And now, from the other side of the frame, Olive could feel something tugging at her, like an invisible thread woven through her rib cage—something that she couldn't help but follow.

In turn, Olive tugged at Morton, who wriggled in her grip like a greased piglet.

Harvey, still in Sir Walter Raleigh mode, waited in front of the painting, his eyes two bright glints in the darkness. "Ready, Your Majesty?"

"Ready." Olive took hold of Harvey's tail and kept her tight grip on Morton's wrist, even though Morton squirmed grumpily. Then, together, the three stepped through the frame and into the even deeper darkness. As her eyes adjusted, Olive picked out a thin strip of moonlight that ran along the bottom edge of an old wooden door. Above it, a round brass doorknob gleamed dully. Olive felt a cool draft rush over her skin as she groped through the alcove for the doorknob and pulled open the heavy attic door.

As soon as a gap appeared, Harvey bolted up the

steps, shouting, "The Ark Raleigh enters the mouth of the Orinoco! Come, men, El Dorado surely lies ahead!"

Olive followed, climbing slowly. She hadn't planned to come back so soon. Without the spectacles, she couldn't get into the attic on her own, and the memory of her long night trapped up there with the snaking, shifting shadows of Aldous McMartin was enough to crush her curiosity down to a nub. In fact, Olive thought she might have lost the nub entirely. But now as she climbed the creaky wooden stairs, she realized that her heart was pounding not with fear, but with excitement. Fear was just the edge that kept the excitement sharp. As she climbed, Olive felt that once again she was being pulled forward, very, very gently, like something at the end of a long, fragile string.

"You can let go now," huffed Morton, managing to yank his hand away from hers at last.

They reached the top of the stairs. The attic was dim, with the round window high above the backyard letting in a beam of moonlight. Olive struck a match and lit the candle she had brought along, tucked in the waistband of her pajamas. In its flickering light, she glanced around at the jumble of furniture and canvases, the circle of mirrors still standing where she had arranged them—and, just as she remembered it, Aldous's tall, paint-spattered easel, draped with a piece of trailing cloth.

Harvey darted forward and bounced from an old sofa into the rafters. "Clear sailing, men! Land ho! Chips ahoy!" he bellowed. "Hoist the mainsail and raise the roof!"

"Not so loud, Harvey!" Olive hissed, but the cat was already leaping out of sight through the shadowy beams.

Olive set the candle down on an old flat-topped steamer trunk. Its gold beams threw wavering shadows against the walls; dark, twisted versions of the sewing mannequins and cabinets and coat trees danced in the corners, looming and fading. Winding her way between the furnishings, Olive headed toward the attic's far corner, where a stack of painted canvases leaned against the wall.

"Morton, come look!" she called softly over her shoulder.

Morton, who had been rolling a small, battered cannon back and forth, got up rather reluctantly and shuffled across the floor to crouch beside her.

They looked through the stack of paintings one at a time, squinting and tilting the canvases, sometimes leaning forward until they accidentally bumped their heads together and gave each other irritated scowls before setting back to work. There were snowy villages and grand manor gardens, peaceful farmyards, and the old wooden barn where Olive first found Baltus, Aldous McMartin's big, mostly friendly dog. But there were no books—at least, not any that they could see from the outside.

"Harvey?" Olive called. "I mean, Sir Walter Raleigh? Can you come and help us, please?"

There was a soft swishing sound from the ceiling, and the cat dropped from the rafters onto the floor before them. "Have you found it, Your Majesty? El Dorado, the golden city?"

"What is he talking about?" said Morton, not quite under his breath.

"Just pretend you understand," Olive whispered back. Then, looking into Harvey's fanatical green eyes, she said, "We might have found it. We just need to look in all of these."

Harvey glanced at the stack of paintings, raised his chin, and sweepingly offered Olive his tail. Olive took it. With her other hand, she held on to Morton, and until the candle in the attic had almost burned out, they climbed in and out of Elsewhere.

They rambled through snowy villages and manor gardens, peaceful farmyards and lonely valleys. They pelted each other with snowballs that dissolved backward into the sparkling drifts, and picked flowers that flew back onto their stems. They were chased by a flock of honking geese who turned out not to be *nearly* as peaceful as they looked. And, in a painting of a willow-lined river, Olive tripped over her own feet and knocked Morton off of his, so that they both splashed face-first into the chilly green water. But nowhere did they find a book of spells.

They crawled back through the frame around the painted river, Harvey flouncing, Olive dripping, and Morton—though he was already completely dry again—scowling violently.

"I'm tired," he announced as Olive wrung the water out of the cuffs of her pajamas and Harvey bounded back toward the rafters, shouting, "Man the man-ropes! Moor the moorings!"

"You don't *get* tired," Olive reminded him.

"I'm tired of *looking*." Morton sat down on the floor and flopped backward against a rolled-up rug. "We've been looking and looking. We've checked every single painting in this stupid old attic, and we haven't found anything."

"But we're so close, Morton," said Olive. "I can tell." Even by the light of the dwindling candle, she could see the skepticism on Morton's face.

"How do you know?"

"I'm not sure, but I can just—I can *feel* it. It's like . . . like the house is guiding me."

Morton looked at her as dubiously as if Olive had

said she'd been taking advice from a ham sandwich.

Olive sighed. "Maybe we missed it somehow. Maybe we need to check these paintings again."

"Well, you can check them again without me."

"But two eyes are better than one," Olive pointed out. "I mean, four eyes are better than two. I mean—"

"It's two *heads*," said Morton. "And besides, if *you* want to find this book so much, you should do it yourself. Paddle your own canoe. That's what Lucy used to say."

"What does that even *mean*?" asked Olive. "And who is Lucy?"

"She's my—" said Morton, and stopped suddenly as a funny look dropped over his face. "She was . . . my sister."

"Morton—you remembered her name!" Olive jumped to her feet. A few droplets of water pattered onto the floor. "Don't you want to find this book, and see if it'll help us find out more? Maybe it has a spell to bring back lost memories, or to make a compass that finds missing people or something!"

Morton paused for a moment. His expression, when he turned to Olive, was hard to read. "Maybe you shouldn't find it," he said.

"What?"

"It belongs to *them*," said Morton. "So . . . maybe you shouldn't find it."

"But the McMartins are gone now," Olive argued. "You *know* that. You were *there*."

Morton stared at her doubtfully, his pursed lips twisting to one side.

"Morton . . ." Olive began, but Morton had hopped up and was stalking away toward the steps.

"I'm not going to look with you anymore," he said over one shoulder. "And I don't think you should look anymore either. Sir Walter?" he called toward the rafters. "Come and take me home."

"Aye-aye, Sir Pillowcase!" Harvey swung from the rafters to the back of an old chair, catapulting off the cushions and landing at Morton's feet. The two of them started down the stairs. Olive had no choice but to grab the candle and hurry after them.

10

OLIVE WAS SO mad at Morton that she didn't even tell him good-bye. The moment he and Harvey began to climb into the frame around the painting of Linden Street, she turned away and trudged into her bedroom. Then she tugged off her wet pajamas, getting even madder when one of the buttons snagged in her hair. Finally she pulled on a dry nightgown and threw herself down on the pillows. Hershel rolled against her face. Olive shoved him away, a bit rudely. She was so angry, she didn't even notice that Horatio had disappeared.

They had been so close—*so close*—and again the book had slipped through her fingers. The tugging sensation that pulled at her from the other side of the attic door felt almost uncomfortable now, like a rubber band that was stretched just a bit too far. Olive wondered what would happen if it broke.

She buried her face in the pillow. Fine. She would look again tomorrow, *without Morton,* if that was the way he wanted it. She would look without Harvey too, if she could. If it weren't for those stupid broken spectacles . . .

The pillow cradled her head, muffling the creaks and taps of the old stone house. Before she knew it, Olive was wandering through the feathery gray mist of almost-sleep, but in the next second, she was wide awake again, flipping over onto her back and staring up at the ceiling in a daze. Something had broken her sleep. Something that still whispered through her mind like a dragon's tail, or the long train of a woman's silk dress.

As she stared up at the ceiling, an image flickered dimly in her mind, parting the fog, coming closer and closer, until she could almost touch it.

It was a book.

A huge, heavy-looking book.

Clasped in a pair of large, bony hands.

She had seen that book somewhere before. She was sure of it. The last wisps of fog parted like a torn cobweb, and all at once, Olive knew exactly where it was.

She scooted off the bed and back into the hallway. The faint light of the predawn sky turned the walls, floor, and paintings varying shades of blue. Her own hands, groping for the bathroom door, were the pale, pearly blue of something drowned. She found the candle and matchbook and tiptoed back out into the hall.

"Sir Walter?" she whispered as loudly as she dared. "Sir Walter Raleigh? Can you hear me?"

Harvey's splotchy head poked out from the open doorway of the pink room, just ahead of her. "Your Majesty?"

Olive hurried along the carpet. "Sir Walter, I think I've found the location of—that place you said. El Dorito."

"The Lost City of Gold?" Harvey whispered back, his green eyes widening. "Downfall of Orellana? Vanquisher of Pizarro?"

"Yes," said Olive quickly. "But we have to hurry. We have to reach it before dawn. Will you take me back up to the attic?"

"Ah, the northern passage. Yes, indeed, Your Majesty! Follow me!" And Harvey whirled around, whisking away into the darkness.

In seconds, they were through the frame, climbing the dusty stairs back to the attic.

"I shall explore the leeward shore!" Harvey announced, bolting into the jumble. Olive barely heard him.

The tugging sensation was stronger and steadier now. She took a deep breath, raised her candle, and let it pull her up the stairs, across the creaking, bug-littered floor, to the spot right in front of Aldous's easel. The cloth covering the easel was thick with dust except where her own fingers had brushed it away. Olive felt a little prickly thrill at the thought that no one had touched it—or anything else in this attic, in fact—for years and years. No one but her.

Olive lifted the cloth with one hand.

Beneath it, waiting on the easel, was the unfinished painting Olive had seen once before. She flinched at the sight of it. She had tried to forget it, but her memory must have filed it away somewhere—perhaps in the same messy, seldom-used drawer where her former phone numbers were jumbled with the rules of several card games and the recipe for apple crisp. Now she looked at it again, matching it with the picture that had trailed through her dreams.

The canvas showed the inside of a blue room. In the foreground, on a dark wooden table, there lay an open book. And wrapped around the book was a pair of long-fingered, bony hands. They were Aldous McMartin's hands. The hands led up to wrists and then ended, suddenly, with a line of jagged paint strokes where Aldous's arms would have been if he had ever finished the painting.

Olive's heart fluttered in her rib cage like a trapped bird. That was the spellbook. There was no question. Aldous had made a safe place for it, and had planned to paint himself right there with it, standing guard over the book. But he must have run out of time. As she stood looking at the book, the pulling sensation got stronger, until it felt almost like gravity, the kind that pulls you down staircases before you can catch hold of the banister.

"Sir Walter?" Olive called, struggling to keep her voice calm. "Come here. I need you."

There was a soft swishing sound from the ceiling, and the cat dropped from the rafters onto the top of the easel. "Command me as you like, Your Majesty," he declared. "I will sail for the colonies. I will battle the Spanish armada. I will—"

"I don't need any of that," said Olive. "I need to get in here."

Harvey craned over the top of the canvas and peered into the painting. "Oh," he said, his voice suddenly small. "I see."

"Can't you do it?"

Harvey looked back up at Olive. When he spoke again, it was in that same small voice. "There is a difference between *can* and *should*."

Olive was surprised. If there was anyone who *didn't* know the difference between *can* and *should*, it was

Harvey. Last month, he had hidden in the branches of a tree near the sidewalk and bombarded everyone who passed by with pinecones while making cannon-blasting sounds. A few weeks later, he had shorted out the wiring in the library chandelier by practicing Robin Hood–style leaps onto the furniture.

"What will happen if we do go in?" Olive asked.

Harvey appeared to think for a moment. It was hard to tell, because he stopped to think so rarely. "Well," he said at last, "that depends on you, really. The only thing that's certain is that *something* will happen."

Olive looked at the painting, at the thick, open book, at the pair of hands lying on it like two giant, pallid spiders. And she wanted it. She had never wanted anything—not a snow day, not a unicorn, not *anything*—so much in her entire life. She wasn't going to think about anything else or do anything else or go anywhere else until she had that book in her hands. She wasn't sure that she *could* go anywhere else. The pulling had gotten so strong, it was hard for her to move even her eyes away.

"Let's get it," she whispered.

Harvey nodded. It was a funny nod—resigned, and a little bit sad. But Olive wasn't paying him much attention.

"We need a plan, though," she rushed on. "I think I have an idea."

Olive didn't tell Harvey this, but it really wasn't *her* idea. The idea dropped into her mind fully formed, like a present—just like the image of the book itself when she woke up from her scrambled dreams. Dragging herself away from the painting, Olive hurried across the room to a pile of boxes stacked in one corner. There was something in those boxes that she was meant to find.

Setting the candle carefully on the floor, Olive flipped open their lids, tossing out stacks of ancient bedsheets, old newspapers, empty picture frames. Finally, in one moldy box, she uncovered an aging scrapbook, its pages crumbling and delicate, its covers held together by a frayed cord. Ordinarily, Olive would have liked to look through the scrapbook, studying the yellowed newspaper articles and old snapshots and pictures from antique fashion magazines, but she was in too much of a hurry to care about any of that just now. She turned it over, mentally measuring its size and shape, and skidded back across the floor to the easel.

"I'm ready," she said. "Let's go."

Wordlessly, Harvey extended his tail for Olive to hold. He dropped from the top of the easel into the painting. Immediately, the hands fluttered, rising up from the book, patting searchingly at their nonexistent arms. The sight made Olive shudder. But she kept her grip on Harvey's tail and clambered into the painting after him. The long-unused bottles of pigment rattled on the easel's shelf as her feet kicked through.

Inside, she nearly slid over the edge of the long wooden table. The room within the painting was small, almost cramped, even with nothing in it but the table, the book, and the hands. The blue walls were bare and windowless. Olive was sure that this was a room Aldous had created just for this painting, to keep the grimoire as safe as it could be. Back on the book now, the hands gave a slight twitch, like animals sensing a disturbance in the air.

Olive sat on the table's edge, taking deep breaths. Gently, she opened the scrapbook and laid it on the table, edge to edge with the spellbook. She glanced down at the scrapbook's pages. Taped beside a row of pressed flowers that had long ago turned brown was a photograph of two girls, their arms linked, their faces framed by curly hair and lacy collars. One was pretty but sour-faced, with dark hair and eyes. The other had lighter hair and a chilly little smile, like something that would melt if it was left out of the refrigerator. Olive recognized both of those faces. In tiny, faded script beneath the picture, someone had written *Annabelle and Lucinda, aged 14.*

The wheels in Olive's head started to turn.

No time for that now! shouted the voice in her head that

controlled the wheels. The spellbook—the treasure she had been searching for, the tool that would change *everything*—was just inches away from her, almost close enough to read. It was exerting a pull so strong, she was surprised that strands of her hair weren't floating toward it, as though it were a static-charged balloon. Between the painted hands on its open pages, she could glimpse scratchy lines of handwritten letters, curls of calligraphy made by someone who had certainly never seen a ballpoint pen. The sight made her heart pound.

"All right," she whispered to the cat crouching beside her. "I need you to cause a distraction. Get the hands off of the book, and I'll slide this one into its place. When I say *go,* we move. Okay?" She glanced down at Harvey, who was staring at the hands as though they might explode. Harvey gave a teeny nod.

"Go."

"Have at thee!" Harvey snarled, pouncing onto the hands, claws out. "Who dares to try his strength against Sir Walter Raleigh?"

Like two giant crabs, the hands jumped from the book and locked around the cat's body.

Olive reached for the spellbook. Before she had even quite grasped it, she felt—or thought she felt—the book leap into her arms, like a cat that is delighted to be let in from the rain. Olive clutched the old book

tight against her body. It was very heavy, with its thick pages and leather cover, and its corners had been softened by years of use until they felt almost like velvet. Olive stroked the edge of its closed pages calmingly. The book seemed to stir deeper into her arms.

"Reee-OW!" Harvey screeched, bouncing up into the air in front of her, the hands still locked around his body. With a start, Olive remembered what she was meant to be doing. But she couldn't bear to put the book down. She didn't want to turn her attention from it, even for a second. Finally, she took one hand away from the book just long enough to push the open scrapbook into its place, and then wrapped her arms tightly around it again. She was almost afraid to look away from it, sure that somehow the book would vanish from her grasp.

"Unhand me, villain!" Harvey shouted, writhing and twisting as the hands tightened around him. "Or you shall feel the wrath of the greatest swordsman in England!"

Olive wasn't listening. As the cat thrashed around on the table, screeching a string of Elizabethan insults ("Thou plume-plucked paper-faced puttock!" Olive thought she heard), she was stroking the edge of the book's thick leather cover, running her fingertips along the spine that felt almost as soft as living skin. She wanted to never let it go.

Harvey made a panicked, choking sound. One of the hands had worked its way around his throat and was steadily squeezing. "Your Majesty . . ." he wheezed.

With a reluctant sigh, Olive tore her eyes away from the book, pinning it firmly to her side with one elbow. It clung to her body like a magnet. "Hold still, Harvey!" she commanded. But Harvey was too hysterical to listen. While he kicked and clawed and gasped for breath, Olive made a wild grab at one of the hands. Its cold, painted skin squirmed in her fist. It felt like a plastic sack of cold jelly, but with bones twisting and moving inside of it. While Olive held on, it wriggled, turning and groping, snaking its fingers between hers. Suppressing a scream, Olive shook her arm, and the hand flew off, hitting the blue wall with a smack. On the floor, it flipped over and scuttled back toward the leg of the table, its bulbous joints working in a blur.

Back on the tabletop, Harvey lay on his back, kicking weakly at the air. "Strike, man, strike!" he croaked.

Keeping the spellbook under her arm so that both her hands were free, Olive pried the remaining hand from Harvey's neck and flung it down on the scrapbook. The hand stilled. It ran its fingertips over the scrapbook's worn pages. The left hand, which had clambered up the table leg, poked at the scrapbook from the other side.

Olive turned back to the spellbook. It was still safe

under her arm, its cover gleaming as softly as silk. "Get us out, Harvey," Olive ordered.

Harvey gave his head a dizzy shake, waited for Olive to grasp his tail, and stumbled back out into the attic.

Safely outside the painting, Olive glanced up at the easel. Inside the canvas, both long, bony hands had curled around the open scrapbook in the very position they had held before. She pressed the heavy spellbook tight to her chest. Her heart pounded against its cover like a fist knocking on a door.

"All right, Sir Walter," she whispered to the cat panting on the floor beside her. "Now let's get out of here."

11

I N THE CORNER of the attic, the little candle had sput-
tered down to a nub. Olive hurried across the floor
to pick it up. By its light, she got her first good look at
the McMartins' book of spells.

Its leather cover was worn to rich amber. It was
covered with bumps and dimples in places, but was as
smooth as glass in others—perhaps where hundreds of
years of hands had rubbed it. Ancient embossing flickered here and there on its surface, like fine threads
sewn into the leather. Olive was so enthralled that she
almost stepped on Harvey, who was waiting for her at
the top of the stairs.

"Hey, Olive," he said, sidling out of the way, "before
we leave, would you . . . would you cover up that painting again?"

Olive glanced back up at the unfinished canvas. The slick sheen of the paint rippled in the candle-light. Aldous's disembodied hands clutched the scrapbook. She hurried to smooth the dusty cloth back into place. The painting disappeared like a stage between a pair of closing curtains.

Harvey didn't speak as they padded down the stairs and back out through the painted arch. He was silent in the pink room, silent in the hallway, and silent in the bathroom, where Olive stopped to leave the dying candle, freeing both hands to clasp the book against her body.

Even when they got back to Olive's bedroom, Harvey didn't say a thing. In the doorway, he made an odd little throat-clearing sound before darting off down the hall, but Olive was too preoccupied with the book to notice. She had the McMartins' spellbook in her hands. Every other thought simply floated away, like bits of fuzz in front of an electric fan.

She slid into her bed, flicked on the tiny reading lamp, and tilted the book up against her knees. It was heavy and almost as wide as Olive's body, but it nestled comfortably in her lap. Horatio and Leopold never nestled that way. Harvey was more likely to joust with a mailbox than to curl up in her lap, even if it meant giving himself a minor concussion in the process.

Gently, Olive stroked the worn leather cover, and

the book seemed to glisten under her fingertips. Then, as she watched, the glinting spots carved into the leather shifted into a familiar shape—a shape so worn and so ornate with its swirls and curlicues and spots of flaking gold that she hadn't recognized it before. It was the letter M.

Olive wiggled her toes beneath the sheets. She felt as if she were about to unwrap a pile of birthday presents, but with the excitement multiplied by a hundred. There wouldn't be any lumpy sweaters, confusingly complicated calculators, or math games with names like Let's Have Sum Fun! inside of *this* surprise.

She took a deep breath, making the moment last. Then she lifted the cover and opened the book.

On the thick yellow frontispiece was a sketch of a tall, nearly leafless tree, done in strokes of dark blue ink.

The tree's trunk was thick and crooked, dividing into a tangle of branches and twigs, all joining and bending and forking. Olive had to squint to see it, but on each branch and twig, a name was written in tiny, pointed letters. Most of them were names she had never seen before: *Athdar McMartin, Ansley McMartin, Aíllil McMartin.* But near the top, in the very center of the tree, Olive found a name she recognized: *Aldous McMartin.* This name branched off toward *Albert McMartin,* and then to *Annabelle McMartin.* The branch from Annabelle went nowhere. It trailed away between the blue leaves at the very top of the page, dwindling into a line so thin that it finally became invisible.

Olive wriggled deeper into her pillows and carefully turned the page.

Sleeping spell. The word *spell* sent a happy little shock down to her toes. Olive skimmed the thick yellow paper. There were lots of words she didn't recognize— *valerian* and *boneset* and *witchnail*—but most of the words were things she knew or sort of knew, like *chamomile* and *nightshade.* Even when the words were familiar, like *cup* or *water* or *bird's wing,* the delicate, thorny calligraphy transformed them into something mysterious and completely new.

The whole first portion of the book seemed to be about sleeping. There were spells to bring sweet dreams and spells to send nightmares and spells to make sleepwalkers fetch things for you. Reading about sleep was making her sleepy. Olive settled down onto her back, holding the book up above her and flipping to the next section. Here were spells that looked more like recipes: potions for winning hearts and erasing memories, a cake that made everyone who ate it angry at each other.

Olive read on, fighting the tiredness that kept threatening to slam her eyelids down. *To Attract Paper Cuts. To Give a Headache. To Cause Uncomfortable Flatulence.* (Olive had to look up that last word in her dictionary.) *To Bring on a Fever. To Break a Bone.* The instructions were getting more and more complicated, full of ingredients she didn't recognize or couldn't imagine gathering—like frogs' tongues. Where would a person get frogs' tongues? Olive knew that some people ate frogs' *legs*, but she'd never seen frogs' tongues in a grocery store . . .

Wait a minute, said a distant, nudging voice from the very back corner of Olive's mind. Wasn't there something she was supposed to be looking for? Olive peeled her eyes away from the book for a moment, glancing around the room. The sky beyond the window was lightening very softly, like deep purple cloth after years of washing. It could have been either dawn or twilight. It looked like the sky in Morton's world.

Morton. Olive jerked upright. That was it. She was

going to find a way to help Morton. Her eyes fell back on the book. But there were so many more pages to go, so many more interesting spells to read . . . There would be plenty of time to think about Morton. She would get to it later.

Olive nestled her head against the pillow and raised the heavy book again. If only she didn't feel so sleepy . . .

Her eyelashes were tugging at her eyelids like a hundred little curtain-pulls. Her arms began to sag. The book slid down, gently, heavily, and came to rest on Olive's rib cage. She breathed in its dusty smell. It smelled like the floor of an antique shop, like ballet slippers hidden in a drawer for years, and like something sharper, like rust or cinnamon. Perhaps like fingerprints left five hundred years ago, in Scotland, in a house that had been turned to ash.

When she fell asleep, it was with the light still on and the open book forming a little roof above her heart. For the rest of the night she wandered through dreams full of trees and clutching hands and blowing paper. In the longest, clearest dream, she was part of the ground—in the ground, or beneath the ground—with a tree growing up out of her heart, its heavy trunk reaching from her toward the sky.

Olive slept and slept and slept. On her chest, the book rose and fell with each breath.

SOMETHING WAS MAKING a thumping sound. Olive nestled deeper into the pillows and squinched her eyes shut. "No thank you," she mumbled. "I don't need a refill."

But the thing kept thumping. Slowly, Olive opened her eyes, and the hamburger and Coke she'd been enjoying dwindled away into her own rumpled bedspread. The book was still open on her chest, her room was drenched with bright yellow sunlight, she was very, very hungry, and a huge bumblebee was thumping its face stubbornly against her window.

Olive glanced at the alarm clock: 12:31, said the red digits. She had never slept so late in her whole life, not even when she'd been delirious with a fever of 104 and thought that her toes had all traded places. No wonder she was hungry.

Dressed in fairly clean shorts and a T-shirt and carrying the spellbook in both arms, Olive stumbled out into the upstairs hall. "Mom?" she called. "Dad?" But the big house was quiet.

She jogged down the stairs, the heavy book thumping against her hip, and craned around the corner toward the shiny carved squares of the library's double doors. "Hello! Anybody home?" Her voice rang against the walls and faded away.

In the kitchen, a note in her mother's handwriting hung on the refrigerator door.

"Good morning, dear," read the note. "Gone to campus. Back between 4:06 and 4:09, depending on traffic and other variables. Help yourself to 1/6 of the leftover lasagna for lunch. Love, Mom and Dad."

Olive decided she'd prefer a big bowl of Sugar Puffy Kitten Bits to figuring out how much one-sixth of the lasagna was. She placed the spellbook on the counter in front of her, poured a heaping bowl of cereal, and sat down on one of the high stools. For a second, she was tempted to offer the book a bite of cereal—but that was silly, of course.

Olive often read while she ate (or ate while she read, as reading was the thing that usually continued both before and after). But this morning, even as hungry as she was, her cereal got pretty soggy. Whenever she tried to turn her attention to her increasingly un-puffy Kitten Bits, the book seemed to tug her back, urging her to read one more word, one more line, one more page. And soon she came to a group of spells that almost made her forget about breakfast entirely.

To Conjure a Familiar, said the first.

Olive skimmed the list of ingredients. It was a horrible spell, involving human blood and a cat's eye, and something that came out of a toad's stomach. When all the ingredients were combined, boiled together on a fire of elder branches under the thinnest crescent moon, a creature would appear, called up from another world to serve its master. Forever.

Her eyes scanned the spell again. So this was how the McMartins had taken possession of Horatio, Leopold, and Harvey. She imagined some long-dead McMartin—perhaps it was Athdar or Aillil, or someone even farther down the trunk of that blue-inked family tree—standing over the red glow of a fire somewhere in the craggy Scottish hills. Olive bumped the cereal bowl aside and pulled the book closer.

To Control Your Familiar, read the next spell. *To Punish Your Familiar.* And, after that: *To Summon Your Familiar.*

The words fit into Olive's mind like a key into an invisible lock. She could almost hear the tick of the bolt pulling back, the gears starting to turn. If she got this spell to work, she might finally be able to explore whatever lay beneath the basement's trapdoor. Leopold wouldn't stand guard over it for no reason; there *had* to be something there, something important, something that would reveal new secrets about the house, the McMartins, or Elsewhere itself. She could use this spell to get Leopold out of the way.

Without taking her eyes off the book, Olive scooped up a spoonful of cereal and chewed distractedly. The steps in the process looked fairly simple; she didn't have to bury anything for six months and dig it up by the light of a full moon (that was one of the instructions she'd seen on another page), and she didn't have to do anything that might accidentally light the house on fire. The spell only required white chalk, milk, "a trace of your familiar: fur or feather, hide or hair," and several unusual plants. Olive had milk and chalk, she could get the fur . . . and she knew where to look for unusual plants.

She thumped her heels against the rungs of the stool, thinking. This spell would be a good place to start experimenting. Maybe it wouldn't even work, and if it didn't, no one would be hurt—nobody had to donate blood to the mixture, no frogs had to lose their tongues. Besides, if you had to experiment on someone, why not experiment on a friend?

On the other hand, if she *did* succeed, she would know that the book worked, and that she was capable of casting other spells. If A equals B, and B equals C, then you can spell *cab* . . . or whatever it was her parents were always saying about causation. Therefore, with a little practice using the spellbook, she would have a better chance of helping Morton.

The thought of Morton clunked to the bottom of Olive's stomach like the reminder of an unpleasant chore. Helping Morton was just one of the many things she could do with this wonderful book. And it would be quite dull and silly to *only* use it for helping Morton. That would be like going to a gigantic buffet and eating only the carrots and celery when a whole dessert table is set up at the end, heaped with cupcakes and cookies and chocolate truffles and soft-serve ice cream just *waiting* in a big silver machine . . .

Olive's stomach rumbled. She took another bite of soggy cereal.

She'd get around to helping Morton eventually. Besides, if Morton hadn't been so unhelpful and stubborn about helping *her* look for the spellbook, maybe she'd feel more inclined to help *him*.

By the time Olive had scooped up the last mooshy bite from the puddle of pink milk at the bottom of the bowl, the microwave clock read 1:22. She had (Olive did some slow and painful math in her head) two hours and eighty-four minutes until her parents came home. Wait—that didn't sound right. Olive subtracted again. Two hours and *sixty*-four minutes. It wasn't much time.

She slid down from her stool, hugging the open spellbook to her chest, and headed toward the basement door. A cool draft of air swirled around her bare toes as she yanked it open. To keep the book out of Leopold's sight, Olive placed it carefully on the top step. As soon as she set the book down, her arms ached to pick it up again. *Just a few seconds,* she told herself—or perhaps she was telling the book. *I'll be right back.* Glancing over her shoulder again and again, Olive edged down into the darkness.

"Leopold?" she called.

"At your service, miss," answered a low voice.

Olive pulled the chain of one of the dusty lightbulbs, and in the corner, a pair of green eyes suddenly settled into a large black face.

Olive sat down in front of the cat. The basement floor was so cold against her legs that she half expected them to freeze to the stone, like when you pressed your tongue to a frosty railing. Leopold studied her calmly.

"How are you, Leopold?" Olive asked, with what she hoped was a casual little smile.

"Fit for duty, miss," said the cat.

"Duty?" Olive repeated, frowning. Then she smacked her forehead, pretending to have just remembered the trapdoor. "Oh, of course! Your *station*." She glanced down at the door's deep edges. "It must get so dull, sitting here all alone, in the same old spot, day after day."

"No, indeed, miss," Leopold argued, his eyes widening. "After all, the price of safety—"

"Is eternal vigilance. I remember." Olive shifted her legs on the chilly floor. Just inches away from her knee, the outline of the trapdoor made a deep slash through the stone. "But you have to get uncomfortable sometimes," she went on. "I mean, wouldn't you like to rub your head against something soft, or have somebody around to scratch between your ears?"

Leopold looked slightly surprised, as though just remembering that he *had* ears. Then he tipped his head to one side. "Well, a soldier doesn't like to complain, miss."

"Of course not." Olive nodded understandingly. "But as long as I'm here . . ." She held out her hand.

Leopold lowered his head and let Olive give his ears a good, long rub. His bright green eyes slid shut, and a deep, boat-motor-ish purr began to rumble up from his chest. Olive could see several strands of sleek black fur clinging to her palm already. She pressed her fingers together to trap them. Then she looked back down at Leopold's blissful face. Maybe it was the trusting way his head was pressed against her hand, maybe it was the sound of his purring, but something made Olive want to give Leopold another chance to let her through the trapdoor on his own.

"Leopold," she wheedled, "could you and I—"

Leopold snapped back into upright position. "No, we couldn't."

"But you don't even know what I was going to say!" Olive protested. "Maybe I was going to say, 'Could you and I throw a big ice cream sundae party down here in the basement for all the centipedes and spiders?'"

Leopold squinted one eye. "Was that what you were going to say?"

"Well, no."

"I didn't think so." Leopold puffed out his chest, looking rather proud of his own perceptiveness.

Olive shifted closer, bringing herself eye to eye with the big black cat. "Leopold, why can't I see what's under the trapdoor?" she asked. "Do you think it would scare me? Do you think it isn't safe for me to see? Is it something that shouldn't be let out? *What*?"

Leopold stiffened. "It's not safe for you to know, miss."

"*Leopold!*" Olive moaned, rocking back on her behind and glaring up at the web-covered ceiling. For a moment, she pondered pushing the cat off of the trapdoor, or even picking him up and throwing him. She wasn't sure if she could lift him off the ground, but she was bigger than he was; if she pushed with all her might, she might be able to slide him off . . . But, no—she couldn't do that. It would be like shoving a policeman. She took a deep breath.

"Leopold, please," she said, keeping her voice as gentle as she could. "I *need* to know what's down there. And I'm not going to give up just because you say *no*."

"Miss . . ." said Leopold, giving her a look that had a little drop of something—was it sadness?—at the very bottom. "Please believe me when I tell you that we are doing what we think is best for you."

"Everyone thinks they know what's best for me," muttered Olive, jumping to her feet and stalking away, with several strands of Leopold's fur still clenched in her fist. She yanked the chain on the lightbulb as hard as she could, leaving the basement in darkness. She didn't even look back over her shoulder to see if Leopold's eyes followed her as she stomped up the stairs. She didn't need to look. She knew they did.

Olive slammed through the basement door into the kitchen with the spellbook safely back in her arms. Then she rolled the strands of black fur into a neat little ball and pushed the ball into her pocket. She had given Leopold one last chance, and he hadn't taken it. Whatever happened next would be his fault. This was *her* house, after all, not his. And this was *her* book. And outside, rustling in the faint, humid breeze, was *her* garden. She wheeled toward the back door. But before she could take a second step, she stopped so abruptly that she nearly lost her grip on the book.

Horatio sat in a shaft of sunlight that spilled

through the kitchen windows, his long orange fur glowing around his body like a fiery halo. He'd been waiting for her.

Olive felt an urge to hide the book from the cat's sharp green eyes. She hugged it to her chest, wrapping both arms around it so that the cover was at least partly obscured. The look on Horatio's face told her just how pointless this was.

"I . . ." Olive began, but Horatio got to his feet at that moment. He took a very small step closer to Olive, his fine white whiskers quivering, his green eyes glowing. Olive stopped speaking. They stared at each other. The silence stretched between them like elastic. Olive braced for it to break, ready for Horatio to hiss or growl or yell, but this didn't happen. Instead, it was Horatio who flinched. He edged away from Olive, keeping his distance.

"I know you don't like to listen to me, Olive," he said softly. His usually sharp voice sounded muzzled, like something in it was being held back. "You would rather make your own mistakes than learn from the terrible mistakes of others. So far, you've been lucky, and you've survived those mistakes—those many, *many* mistakes."

Olive opened her mouth, but Horatio went on before she could interrupt.

"Now, you can either keep being lucky, or you can

start being smart. And you can only control one of those things, Olive. I hope that you'll make the right choice."

Then, as Olive watched, the huge orange cat trotted silently past her into the shady hallway.

Olive wavered, turning back and forth between Horatio's retreating backside and the waiting back door, like the needle on a broken compass. The weight of the book leaned against her ribs. All the doubts she'd pushed to the corners of her mind popped out again, arguing in a storm of bossy little voices. She looked down at the book. Horatio's deserted sunbeam coasted over the worn leather, tracing threads of fire in the gold letter M.

M for Mine, Olive told herself.

And then, amid that storm of voices, Olive felt the one force that she was waiting for—a gentle but insistent tugging that started in her chest. It tugged patiently, like a piece of dental floss around a loose tooth. It was the same sort of tugging she'd felt in the attic, leading her toward the painting on the easel. Now it was leading her somewhere else. With a first hesitant step, and then another and another, Olive let the house guide her over the kitchen tiles to the back door, across the porch, and down the steps into the waiting garden.

Standing at the edge of the overgrown garden, Olive could almost see the trapdoor creaking open before her. Somewhere in this bushy chaos lay the key to opening it. In fact, Olive realized with an excited little heart-hop, now that she had the spellbook, the garden might open a lot of doors that she hadn't even known were locked. Over her shoulder, the old stone house loomed, watching her.

Apart from Mrs. Dunwoody's occasional weed-watering, nobody had done a thing to the garden since old Ms. McMartin died. If anything, it looked even more jumbled and lush than it had last month. The plants with purple velvet leaves and the plants with little toothy mouths were still there, along with flowers that looked like staring eyes, and berries that

looked like sacs of spider's eggs. Amid the mess, Olive thought she recognized the twisty green sprout that had given her a welt when she tried to pull it up. She also recognized parsley, because it always came next to the dill pickle with grilled cheese sandwiches. Everything else was a leafy mystery.

She knelt down, careful not to put her knees on anything that might leave thorns in her skin, and opened the book back to the spell for summoning a familiar. In addition to the milk and chalk, she needed to find catnip, thorntooth, nettle, and bat berry. Nettles sting, as Olive was well aware—she had stumbled into more than one patch of them while wandering daydreamily through the woodsy parts of parks—and catnip must smell good, at least to cats. Maybe it smelled like tuna. Olive leaned over a patch of bushy stems, inhaling deeply. She could smell mint and dirt and something that reminded her of the taste of blood when you licked it away from a paper cut, but no fish.

As she crawled to the right, still sniffing, there was a gentle, almost imperceptible twitch from the lilac hedge nearby. Olive stopped sniffing. She leaned back on her heels, carefully pulling the book behind her back, where it couldn't be seen. She scanned the row of lilac bushes. The leaves were too thick for her to see what had moved—if it was a lurking cat, or Mrs. Nivens spying on her, or just a breeze that had stopped at the edge of the lilacs. But the hedge didn't move again. Perhaps it had been her imagination.

And then, just when she was about to turn back to her task, the lilac branches bent and crackled, and Rutherford Dewey stepped through the hedge into her backyard.

"I see you've found the grimoire," he said, brushing a lilac twig off of his rumpled blue dragon T-shirt.

Olive felt her heart jump so high into her throat she was afraid it would get stuck behind her uvula. She swallowed to push it back down. "Were you *spying* on me?" she hissed.

"*Spying* implies that I was watching you without you knowing it." Rutherford jiggled back and forth in his loafers. A lilac leaf, stuck in his messy curls, jiggled back and forth too. "But now you know that I was watching you, and as I was never trying to keep it a secret, I think it can be said that I *wasn't* spying on you."

Olive would have liked to argue with this, but she had no idea how. Instead, she just pulled the book tight against her back and scowled up at Rutherford in her most unwelcoming manner.

Rutherford wasn't daunted.

"Do you think the grimoire is functional?" he asked, moving closer to the garden, speaking so fast that Olive had to replay his words in her head, in slow motion. "Have you experimented with any spells yet?"

For a moment, Olive pressed her hand against the book's open pages while her thoughts skittered around, getting nowhere. It was too late to lie. Rutherford had already seen too much.

"No," she said at last, sounding rather pouty. "I haven't. I'm looking for some ingredients, and then *maybe* I'll try it. But I don't know if I will."

Rutherford dropped down onto his knees next to her, making Olive wriggle a few inches away. "What exactly are you looking for?"

Without speaking, Olive pulled the book around her body and plopped it between them. She pointed to the list of plants.

"Interesting," murmured Rutherford. "Catnip, nettles . . . But I've never heard of bat berry. How will you identify it?"

"Something that looks like a bat, I guess," Olive answered. "Or like something a bat would eat."

Rutherford nodded. "And do you have a hypothesis about thorntooth?"

Olive shrugged. "I was just going to look for something that seems thorny. Or toothy."

"Very logical," said Rutherford with approval. "Of course, you may have to experiment several times, in multiple combinations, in order to limit the variables."

Olive blinked at him.

"Do you want to do the nettles, or should I?" he asked, leaning over the clumps of plants.

Olive opened her mouth to tell Rutherford that *she* should do the nettles, and *he* should work on minding his own business, but she didn't get the chance. At that moment, a voice hooted, "Rutherfooord!" and in the next moment, Mrs. Dewey was hustling past the corner of the big stone house toward the garden. Olive's heart gave a panicky leap. Had Mrs. Dewey been watching them through the hedge? And, if she had, how much had she heard? Olive just had time to flip the spellbook shut and sit on it before Mrs. Dewey's snowman-shaped shadow was falling over them.

"Rutherford Dewey!" Mrs. Dewey puffed. She glanced at Olive, and her mouth turned into a tiny pink smile. "Oh, hello, Olive dear," she said. The smile disappeared like a popped bubble. "Rutherford Dewey, what have I told you about leaving those models of yours all over the dining room floor?"

"You didn't move them, did you?" said Rutherford. "They're all set up for a reenactment of the Battle of Bosworth."

"I nearly broke my neck on them!" said Mrs. Dewey. "I want you to go home right now and put them where they belong."

"Can I have just a little bit longer?" said Rutherford. "We're in the middle of something very important."

"Very important?" Mrs. Dewey repeated skeptically. Her round blue eyes wandered over to where Olive was sitting, and lingered for just a moment on the thing that Olive was sitting on. Olive felt her skin go rigid. Then Mrs. Dewey sighed, and her eyes trailed back to her grandson.

"What exactly are you up to, Rutherford?"

"It's a science experiment. We're trying to identify some unusual plants."

"Oh?" Mrs. Dewey tilted her round head. "What are you looking for?"

"We're looking for something called *bat berry*," said Rutherford. Olive flashed him a look of horror. Rutherford ignored her. "That's not its scientific name, of course, but that's all we have to go on."

Mrs. Dewey tugged up her dress so that the hem was just above her dimply white knees, and then she knelt between them at the edge of the garden. "Let me see," she murmured. Her equally dimply hands rustled through a patch of leaves. "Ah, yes. Here we are." There was a little snap, and Mrs. Dewey held up a black stalk covered with tiny blue berries, all coated by fine silvery hair. "Bat berry," she said.

"What about thorntooth?" said Rutherford.

Olive gave him another horrified look, which was all she could do. She was afraid to speak or to move even a half inch and find Mrs. Dewey's eyes on her—or on the spellbook—again. Why wouldn't Rutherford just *go away*?

"Well, that's this, of course." Mrs. Dewey smiled, plucking a bit of the plant with little toothy mouths. "Anything else?"

"Just a few common things," said Rutherford. "Catnip and nettles."

That was everything. Now Mrs. Dewey had heard practically the entire recipe, and it wouldn't take a huge leap for her to figure out that there was more going on here than Rutherford was admitting. Behind Mrs. Dewey's wide backside, Olive scowled furiously at Rutherford. He merely blinked back at her. Then he gave a little shrug.

"Catnip looks a lot like mint; some people even call it catmint," said Mrs. Dewey. "And the trick with nettles is to use a glove or a tool of some kind—or to very carefully pull it out at the roots. There. See? No stings at all." She dropped the last two specimens beside the bat berry and thorntooth.

"Thank you, Grandma," said Rutherford.

Mrs. Dewey slowly got back to her feet, which were tiny and made a very precarious-looking pedestal for the hefty shape balanced on top of them. "Well," she said, smiling again, "good luck with your experiments." She gave them a last glance—one that Olive was sure took in the badly hidden book—and teetered away toward the front yard.

"Why did you tell her what I was looking for?" whispered Olive through her teeth as soon as Mrs. Dewey was out of earshot.

"She knows a lot about plants," said Rutherford sensibly.

"But now she knows *everything!* She'll suspect something for sure. She probably already knows what I'm doing. She was looking at the book, and—"

Rutherford shook his head. "Why would she suspect anything? I'm always doing experiments and collecting things."

Olive jumped up, grabbing the spellbook. She brushed at its cover furiously, wiping away bits of dirt and grass. "If she thought she was just helping us identify plants, why would she *pick* them? Why, if she didn't know we were going to use them *in* something?"

"I think you're being paranoid," said Rutherford, getting to his feet. "That means you have excessive or irrational fears."

"I know what pear-annoyed is!" shouted Olive, a bit dishonestly. "And I am not being it. Why would your grandmother know so much about these weird plants if she wasn't—" Olive stopped. This argument didn't sound like her. This sounded like someone else. Someone familiar . . . someone furry and splotchily colored and *full* of irrational fears. *She is not what she seems,* Harvey's voice whispered in the back of her mind. *Neither of them is.*

Olive shook her head, erasing the words. Rutherford stood still, watching her, his brown eyes wide and steady behind their dirty glasses. He certainly didn't look like a spy—unless spies looked like small, messy guests at a Dungeons and Dragons convention.

"When are you going to complete your experiments?" Rutherford asked, beginning to jiggle from foot to foot again.

Not while you're around, thought Olive. She shrugged, taking a casual glance at the sky. The sun was still quite high, but it had begun its slow slide toward the horizon, and its light was changing from white to warm gold. Her parents would be home any minute. "I don't know," she said, bending down to gather up the herbs Mrs. Dewey had picked, careful not to touch the nettle's stinging hairs. "I just wanted to see if I could find the right plants, really. I might not try the spell at all."

She glanced at Rutherford's face, wondering if he believed her, and found that he was watching her with a gaze that was even more intent than usual. Olive got the sense that he wasn't just watching her, but *studying* her. His eyes flashed back and forth between her face and the book in her arms.

"I'll be interested to hear how it goes," he said at last. Then he added, almost as an afterthought, ". . . Whatever you decide, I mean."

Then Rutherford turned away and rustled back through the lilac hedge. Olive stood by herself in the garden, holding the book and the bundle of plants, wondering why she felt as though her toes were balanced on the edge of something very, very high.

14

"Is there something wrong with your casserole, Olive?" asked Mrs. Dunwoody as the three Dunwoodys sat around the dinner table a few hours later. "You've eaten nearly fifty percent less than usual."

"I would have said forty percent less," said Mr. Dunwoody, looking interestedly at Olive's plate.

"Forty? I think you would be underestimating there, dear," said Mrs. Dunwoody gently. "I count seventeen noodles remaining on Olive's plate, and at least twenty-two peas, under a proportionately large amount of tuna."

"Yes, I see your point, darling, but I would have said that the amount of tuna looked *dis*proportionately large . . ."

Olive stared into the distance, toward the ivy-curtained window. It was getting dark outside, so she couldn't quite see through the glass. All she could see was the reflected image of her parents, deep in discussion, and her own dazed, motionless face floating between them. But she wasn't really looking at the window at all. In her mind, the trapdoor was creaking open and thudding shut over and over again, so loudly that she was surprised the noise wasn't leaking out her ears. Naturally, this made it very hard to concentrate on tuna casserole.

Furthermore, the minute she'd left the spellbook in her room, hidden under her fuzzy blue bathrobe, she'd felt the tugging begin again. It pulled at her like an invisible cord, yanking harder and harder as Olive moved away, back down the stairs, through the hallway, and into the kitchen to help set the table for dinner. The farther away she went, the harder it tugged, until it was impossible to think about anything else at all.

Her hands itched to hold the book. Her feet jiggled under the table, ready to race up the stairs with or without the rest of Olive's body, and a tingly, nervous feeling kept creeping up and down her arms.

"May I be excused?" Olive asked.

"Certainly, Olive dear," said her mother with a concerned little frown. "Are you feeling all right?"

"I'm fine. I'm just tired," said Olive.

"Sweet dreams, Olive," said Mr. Dunwoody, giving Olive's hair a gentle stroke.

Her parents were already so deep in a continuing discussion of proportions that they didn't even notice when Olive took her unfinished glass of milk up the stairs.

Olive kept both eyes on the glass, concentrating on not spilling. When she reached the painting of Morton's Linden Street just outside her bedroom door, she hurried past, hardly giving it a glance.

As soon as she pushed open the door, the tugging sensation relaxed just a little. Olive left the glass of milk on the dresser and rushed to the bed, where she pulled the book out from beneath her bathrobe. Immediately, a sense of happy relief washed through her. It felt as though she'd been holding her breath for as long as she could stand it, and was now taking a big gasp of fresh air. Olive flopped onto the bed and held the book close. Hershel rolled against her back in a friendly way, but Olive ignored him. She pressed her nose to the spellbook's leather cover, inhaling its dusty, spicy smell, mixed with the minty scent of the herbs, which stuck out between its pages like a bushy bookmark. And she waited.

Downstairs, the voices of Mr. and Mrs. Dunwoody twined through the sounds of silverware against plates, and then were half drowned in the rush of water from the kitchen sink. Olive listened. She hadn't turned on any lights in her bedroom—if her parents peeped in, she wanted them to think she'd gone to sleep—and the violet sky beyond the windows was scattered with the first small sprinkling of stars. The softness of the bed and the warm weight of the book in her arms were pulling her toward sleep. Olive even dozed off once or twice, wandering in dreams through an overgrown garden where one grand, blue tree towered over her, its lowest branches seeming to reach out to her, inviting her to climb up and up and up toward the canopy that spread above her like a leafy, rustling sky—and then she jerked awake, wondering how she had gotten back to her own bedroom.

Olive pinched her arm with her fingernails. She tried counting sheep to stay awake, but she kept losing track somewhere between sixty and eighty, and the sheep kept turning into cats: orange, black, and splotchily colored cats who ran away, refusing to be counted. It was irritating. Then she remembered that counting sheep was supposed to help you fall asleep, not stay awake. At last, two sets of footsteps thumped along the hall below her, and Olive heard the double doors of the library click shut.

She wriggled off the bed and peered out into the hall, making sure no cats or parents were in sight. Then she turned on her bedside lamp and opened the spellbook to the marked page. The spiky calligraphy stood out sharply against the yellowing paper. For a moment, Olive hesitated. She could almost feel the walls of the old stone house leaning in around her, watching. Her heart was beating hard and fast inside her ribs. She couldn't stop now, without ever knowing if the spell would work, without ever seeing what was hidden beneath the basement's trapdoor . . .

With a last look around her dim bedroom, Olive leaned down to read the steps of the spell one more time. And, as she read, a sense of certainty came over her. It closed around her like armor, pressing the last traces of nervousness down into a tiny fire that jumped with her heartbeat. By the time she started to carry out the instructions, Olive was moving so smoothly and confidently that she hardly felt like herself at all.

A glass bowl of stale potpourri stood on her vanity. Olive dumped out the brown petals and set the empty bowl next to the glass of milk. Then she dug through her drawers full of art equipment, pushing aside the palettes of watercolors and the tattered packets of colored pencils until she found a box of chalk. She took out the white piece and set it next to the bowl. The ball of black fur was still safe in her pocket, and now Olive placed it in the bottom of the empty dish.

Moving slowly to keep the door from squeaking, Olive opened her closet. She shoved piles of shoes and books out of the way, clearing the scuffed hardwood floor. With the chalk, she drew a circle on the floor-boards, making sure to leave no gaps or cracks. In the center of the circle, she wrote the name Leopold, in handwriting that was much stronger and spikier than usual. She crumbled the plants around the borders of the circle, gasping now and then when the nettles stung her. Finally, inside the circle's top edge, she set down the glass bowl with its pinch of black fur and filled it with her leftover milk.

Beyond her bedroom door, something creaked.

Olive froze. But whatever had creaked didn't do it again. It was probably just the house settling, Olive told herself, not one of the cats standing outside her room, listening . . . Still, Olive backed out of the closet and shut the door, breathing harder, feeling all the little hairs on her arms standing on end. *What are you so afraid of?* she asked herself. Unfortunately, she also knew the answer to that question.

She was afraid that the spell might not work—or worse, that it might go terribly, hideously wrong. What if it hurt Leopold? What if it made him disappear, and she could never get him back again? What if she couldn't control the spell, and it summoned all three cats, and scrambled all the parts of them together into three insane Frankenstein cats, one with three tails, one with six eyes, and one with nothing but ears all over his body? She imagined Horatio yelling at her out of three mouths at once. The thought made her feel sick to her stomach.

You're letting your imagination run away with you again, said a reasonable voice in her head—a voice that sounded a lot like her father's. *Those things probably won't happen.*

Olive chewed on the inside of her cheek, thinking. The cats seemed able to get in and out of almost anything: closed windows, locked doors, paintings. Even if she *was* able to summon him from the basement, a closet might not hold Leopold. Then again, it might give her the few minutes she needed to get into the basement and through the trapdoor before anyone saw her. Olive dragged her bedside table in front of the closet door, and, just to be safe, her vanity chair too. She backed a few steps away.

Olive took a long, slow breath, imagining the air coming out through the tips of her fingers. She took a last glance at the book lying open on her bed, its spiky letters like delicate black thorns. Then she planted her feet wide apart on the creaking floorboards. *"Leopold,"* she whispered. *"Leopold. Leopold."*

There was a muffled snapping sound from inside the closet.

Olive waited, holding her breath. Then, from behind the stacked furniture and the closed closet door, there came a tiny, mournful mew. Olive had never heard

Leopold—or any of the cats, for that matter—make a sound like this. It squeezed her heart like a little lasso. But the lasso wasn't strong enough to hold her.

The spellbook tugged at her too, but Olive knew this might be her only chance to find out what waited beneath the basement. She gave the book a last, loving glance before tucking it under her blankets. It would be safe there until she came running back.

Olive tiptoed down the stairs. Her parents were hard at work in the library; she could hear the quick clatter of computer keys. There was not a cat in sight in the hallway, or through any of the open doors, all the way to the kitchen. She snatched the trusty camping lantern from one of the high cabinets. Then she raced back across the kitchen floor and plunged down into the darkness of the basement.

The basement air was cool and still. With no light leaking in from upstairs, it seemed even darker than usual. Olive felt her skin shriveling along her bare arms, as if it were trying to run away. She yanked at the strings of the hanging lightbulbs. Shadows slithered into the corners, hiding beneath the stairs, along the edges of mottled stone walls. Where Leopold's flickering green eyes usually appeared, there was no one—only the faint outline of a square door sunk into the chilly stone floor.

It had worked.

Olive dropped to her knees in front of the trapdoor. Her hands shook. Her heart began an excited drum-roll.

She grasped the looped iron handle. The trapdoor was heavy and stubborn, and once it slipped out of her grasp, slamming back down with a thud that seemed to echo beneath the floor. Olive froze, listening, but her parents didn't appear to have noticed. She worked her fingers through the loop this time, braced her legs, and pulled at the door with all her might. Its hinges made an angry sound, like a very old man clearing his throat. Olive leaned the door back as far as it would go, so that it balanced at an angle on its hinges. Then she turned on the camping lantern, held it over the gaping darkness, and took her first timid peek into the space below.

A RICKETY WOODEN LADDER dwindled down from
the trapdoor into the darkness. The shelf where
Aldous McMartin's ashes had been stored waited
beside the ladder, bare now but for a thick coat of
grit and the dusty lace of spiderwebs. Below the shelf,
Olive could glimpse packed dirt walls with wooden
braces running up to the tunnel's ceiling, like the rafters in a mine. The only mine Olive had ever been in
was at an amusement park, where you could ride little
miners' carts up and down underground hills through
stalactites made of sparkly Styrofoam. That tunnel
looked very different from this one. Just kneeling at
its entrance, Olive caught the sensation of something
waiting beneath the old stone house—something real,
something so big that its gravity was pulling her in.

Half of Olive wanted to slam the trapdoor and run back upstairs. The other half wanted to hurry down into the tunnel and explore before anyone could stop her. But both halves knew that if she turned back now, she would regret it. The question of what waited beneath the trapdoor would dig at her relentlessly, like an itch in the middle of her back, just out of reach. After a long moment, Olive reached into the hole and set the camping lantern on the shelf where Aldous's urn had stood. Then, cautiously, she lowered herself onto the first rung of the ladder.

The wood creaked beneath her. She eased onto the next rung, feeling the old wood bend and settle. While she could still reach it, she grabbed the lantern, then jumped the last few feet to the floor. The drop was farther than she'd thought. She landed hard on both bare feet, stumbled forward, and managed to catch her balance just in time to keep from falling flat on her face—or on the lantern, which would have been worse.

If the basement was cold, the tunnel below it was *frigid*. Olive's shorts and T-shirt suddenly felt much smaller and thinner than they had before. Her bare feet, pressed against the freezing dirt, were already turning numb. She shivered, holding both arms tight against her rib cage. The air in the tunnel was damp, tinged with a faint sick-sweet scent of decay. Olive stood between the packed dirt walls, in the change-less chill, and realized that this must be what it feels like at the bottom of a grave. But graves were only six feet deep. This was much deeper. And darker. And colder.

The lantern made a pale splotch on the walls and floor around her. Beyond that splotch, there was only darkness. Olive took a step forward. The splotch of light moved with her, and the darkness resolved itself around it, pouring into the spots that the light had left behind.

She glanced back at the trapdoor. In a Sherlock Holmes story, the trapdoor would slam shut, and she would be stuck down here, with no one near enough to hear her screams. The thought made Olive's skin crawl. But the trapdoor was still open. Olive pressed her back to the wall so that nothing could sneak up behind her. Then she ventured forward, moving faster, following the tideline of the light.

The lantern's glow couldn't reach the end of the tunnel. As Olive headed toward the darkness where everything disappeared, she wondered why Aldous McMartin had built this place. Maybe he had used it to sneak into his neighbors' yards, kidnapping chil-dren, luring people out of their beds. Maybe he had used it to hide awful things, like the catacombs she'd read about beneath the big stone churches in Europe.

Maybe it was some sort of underground tomb for storing all the leftover bits of the McMartin family, everything that used to lie below the headstones that built the basement walls. Maybe bones were stacked up in teetering piles, maybe skeletons were lying on shelves, maybe big pyramids of skulls stood staring, just waiting for Olive to come bumbling along. Knowing her, she'd trip over a heap of bones, smash the lantern, and be stuck down here in total darkness for weeks until—

Don't think like that, said the reasonable voice in her head. *Just keep walking.*

Olive's mouth felt dry and sticky, like the gummy stuff on the back of a price tag. She could only take tiny, shallow breaths.

Pale roots hung from the ceiling in places, as fine as human hair. Once they brushed Olive's head, and for a moment she was sure that her heart had stopped beating. *That's it,* she could almost hear her heart saying. *I can't take it anymore. You're on your own.* But nothing moved, and there was no sound. In a moment, Olive felt the familiar knocking beat behind her breastbone again. She ventured on.

The lamp trembled in her hand, sending twisted, shadowy versions of herself racing over the packed dirt walls. Somehow, these other Olives didn't make her feel any less alone. But she kept going, slowly, following the light, until the roots began to disappear. The ceiling was getting higher too—or the floor was getting lower. Either way, the tunnel was widening until the lantern light didn't reach the walls at all. The air grew even colder and very, very still; Olive couldn't feel the little breezes made by her own motion bouncing back toward her anymore. And suddenly, the farthest edge of the lamplight struck something—something that glimmered back.

Olive hesitated, shivering, wondering if she really wanted to find out what lay ahead. She could still turn back. She could apologize to Leopold and tell him that whatever he was guarding was still secret and safe. She could pretend that none of this had ever happened.

And then, as she stood frozen in the pool of lamplight, Olive felt something she couldn't explain. A funny sensation trickled through her body almost as though it were flowing down the tunnel toward her. Her heartbeat slowed. Her breath drifted out in a long white plume. She didn't feel alone anymore. Instead, Olive felt as though something protective and familiar had wrapped itself around her. She was standing at the very root of the house. Above her, the basement, the gleaming hardwood hallway, the wide stairs, the bedrooms, and the shadowy attic soared up like the trunk of a giant, immovable tree. She was part of that tree now. And once you are part of something, it can't really frighten you.

Raising the lantern, Olive stepped toward the glimmering thing. It grew brighter as her light glinted from a thousand surfaces at once, refracting like the image in a fly's magnified eye. Reflected stripes and glowing circles made weird patterns in the darkness.

The tunnel had ended in a three-sided room. Each of the three walls was covered with shelves, and each shelf was lined with jars . . . hundreds and *hundreds* of jars.

Olive took a careful look all around, turning in a circle. The walls here were stone-lined, like in the basement, except that there were no gravestones here, as far as she could tell. A few thick wooden pillars speared up from the floor, meeting the ceiling that hung several feet above her head. In the center of the room was a long, high table. The whole point of this room, obviously, was the jars. But what *was* this—some ultra-special, top-secret pantry?

Her bare feet whispered across the stones. Once she reached the far wall, she realized that some of the jars were empty, but a few dried streaks of whatever they'd held still clung to their sides, as though they'd been poured out and shoved back into place. Other jars had been smashed. Fragments of murky glass littered the shelves' edges. Olive walked very carefully, avoiding the shards that were scattered across the floor. Faint stains lingered here and there on the stones.

On tiptoe, she took hold of a jar on the topmost shelf. Its thick bluish glass had grown cloudy with time, and Olive rubbed it with the heel of her hand. Inside, something dried and flaky crumbled from the jar's walls, like old milk around the rim of the jug. Olive shook the jar. The white flakes moved and settled.

Bouncing on both feet for warmth, Olive took down another jar. This one was full of something reddish and powdery that looked a bit like cinnamon. The next one contained tiny blue-black curls that might have been petals from a flower. Another one was filled with thick yellow liquid. As Olive turned the jar, clearing it off with her palm, a small skull appeared between her spread fingers. In the first moment of surprise, Olive nearly dropped the jar. Then she swallowed hard and held it toward the lantern, turning it to see what was inside. A bird skeleton floated in the yellow liquid, its wings bare of feathers, as delicate as paper lace. She shoved the jar back into place.

The cold was becoming painful now. Olive's arms felt like pieces of raw chicken straight out of the refrigerator. Determined to stay for as long as she could stand it, she skimmed along the lower shelves.

In the unbroken jars were things that looked like dried leaves, and things that looked like mold, and things that looked like nothing she had ever seen before— probably because they were meant to be inside the body of something else. When she came to something that was definitely a jar full of dead spiders, Olive bit her tongue to keep from screaming out loud.

She backed toward the high wooden table, shivering, keeping one eye on the jars in case anything in them started to move. The table's surface was cluttered with empty jars and lids, sheets of thick yellowed paper, and old dried-up pens. A few big stone bowls with funny rounded mallets sat there as well. Olive dipped her fingertip carefully into one of these bowls. It came away covered with bright orange powder.

Wiping her finger on her shorts, Olive squinted down at one of the sheets of paper. *Carmine,* it said. Nothing else. Olive frowned. Carmine? Was that somebody's name? She turned over the other sheets of paper. They were blank. But hidden beneath them were scraps of other pages, all torn into tiny bits. Someone had ripped up a sheaf of papers and then hidden them, like Olive sometimes did with a test that had gone particularly badly. What were these? Recipes?

Olive glanced up at the rows and rows of jars, each reflecting a thin band of lantern light. Then she looked back down at the table. And *then,* for the first time, she noticed something else that glimmered. Something closer, and smaller, and very familiar.

Olive stopped. Everything else stopped too—her breathing, her blinking, her blood moving slowly around in her chilly body. Because there, on the table, half hidden behind a large empty jar, was a pair of spectacles.

They were bigger than Ms. McMartin's spectacles, which Olive had found in a dresser drawer so many weeks ago, and which she had crushed in the upstairs hallway when she fell out of the forest painting. They looked heavier, sturdier, as if they were made of a tougher metal. Annabelle McMartin's spectacles, with their thin frames and long, delicate chain, had been the spectacles of a woman. These were the spectacles of a man.

These were Aldous McMartin's spectacles.

Olive's thoughts exploded like a giant firework, shooting every worry away. Delight, excitement, and freedom surged through her, along with something even more wonderful, something like hearing your shovel thud against a chest of treasure you had buried yourself and thought you'd never find again. She reached for the spectacles.

"Olive!"

Olive whirled around. Some instinctive part of her brain made her hide the spectacles behind her back.

All three cats stood in the entrance to the stone chamber. By the pale light of the camping lantern, they appeared silvery and blurred, with only their green eyes flashing clearly against the background of darkness. Horatio was the one who had spoken. Behind him, Harvey glowered up at her. Leopold hung back at the light's edge, his shoulders slumped and his head hanging low. If Olive didn't know it was impossible, she would have sworn that the black cat was crying actual tears.

"I hoped it wasn't true," said Horatio softly. He remained at the edge of the stones, as if he didn't want to come any nearer to Olive. "But, once again, I was wrong to place my hope in you."

Olive's stomach, which had been floating with ecstatic butterflies just a moment ago, began sinking toward her right kneecap.

"The moment you're out of one danger, you're off looking for another, aren't you? And you're not just putting yourself in jeopardy, but everyone around you, everyone who cares most about you. But you seem to conveniently forget about this—to forget, or not to care."

Olive opened her mouth to protest, but Harvey let out a hiss like a rattlesnake, his teeth glinting in the lantern light. Olive took an involuntary step back.

"You had to push farther, didn't you," Horatio went on, in the same quiet voice. "Now you're trying to *control* us, when we have risked our safety, again and again, to protect *you*?"

Leopold made a noise that sounded almost like a sob. Harvey leaned against him protectively and glared at Olive.

Olive's stomach headed for her big toe. "I don't see why you thought you had to protect me from *this,*" she said, gesturing toward the rows of jars and trying to smile. "A giant pantry? What's so scary about that?"

The cats' eyes widened. They exchanged rapid glances. None of them spoke.

"And besides," said Olive, an indignant feeling slowly building itself up to a fire inside her, "the spellbook is mine now. Why can't I use it?"

"That book is using *you,*" said Horatio.

Olive's mouth fell open. "It is not."

Horatio blinked up at her. "Do you know what a witch is, Olive?"

Several pictures zoomed through Olive's mind: pointy black hats, broomsticks, a young Annabelle McMartin smiling sweetly from her portrait. Nothing that made for a very good answer.

Fortunately, Harvey didn't wait for one. "A witch is someone who uses magic," he snapped, in a voice Olive hardly ever heard: his own. But angrier.

"Don't you see what's going on?" asked Horatio. "You're becoming one of them."

Olive shook her head, slowly at first, then faster, until the room was a blur. "No," she said. "I'm not . . . like them."

"Is that so?" Horatio raised his whiskery eyebrows. "What do you call using the McMartins' things? Harvesting their plants, casting their spells? What do you call making Leopold obey you, against his will?" Leopold made another little choking sound. "What do you call making Harvey help you to get that ridiculous book and using it, in spite of his warnings?"

"I didn't *make* Harvey do it," Olive objected. "He could have said no."

Harvey let out another low hiss. "Once you asked for it, I had to," he spat. "The house wanted to give it to you."

"We've tried to protect you." Horatio's eyes narrowed, becoming sharp slits of reflected light. "But it appears you're not on our side anymore, Olive. If this goes any farther, it will be us *against* you. Either way, from now on, you're on your own."

Horatio turned, the tuft of his tail vanishing into the darkness like the fronds of some undersea plant. Leopold followed him, hanging his head. Harvey went last, giving Olive a long, hard look that left her frozen in place for several cold minutes after the cats had gone.

And then she was truly alone.

16

CLUTCHING THE PAIR of spectacles and the camping lantern, Olive struggled to the top of the ladder, hoisted herself through the trapdoor, and hurried up the basement steps. The cats had already disappeared.

She left the lantern in its place on the cabinet shelves. Her parents were still shut inside the library, and they didn't seem to hear her as she raced up the staircase into her bedroom, shivering, and threw herself under the covers, new spectacles, clothes, and all. She grabbed the book, which lay just where she'd left it underneath the blankets, and held it tight to her chest. Immediately, she felt a little bit warmer, and much less alone.

The gold embossing flickered in the light of her bedside lamp. Olive snuggled up against the smooth leather cover and fought to push down the lump that kept rising in her throat. *Stupid cats,* she told herself. Who needed them anyway? She had her own pair of spectacles again. If they wanted to pretend to be in charge of this house, let them. Olive knew who had the real power. This was *her* house.

She buried her face against the book's velvety pages, wrapped her fingers tight around the spectacles, and waited for sleep or morning, whichever came first.

By the time Olive woke, her room was filled with searing sunlight. In her sleep, she'd wriggled all the way underneath the covers, wandering through dreams of forests and blowing leaves and high, thorny hedges that kept growing and growing, no matter how hard she tried to push through. Olive stretched, wondering why she felt as though she'd hardly slept at all. Her legs hurt, and her back hurt, and her fingers were cramped and sore from being wrapped around the spectacles all night.

The spectacles! Olive gave a happy gasp, remembering all the exploring that lay ahead of her—and then she froze, halted by something that *didn't* lay beside her.

The spellbook was gone.

Olive put the spectacles into the pocket of her shorts and shoved away the rumpled blankets, searching every corner of the bed. She found a pink sock that she'd been missing for weeks and a blue gumball, now covered with a fine fur of lint, but no book. She bent over the edge of the mattress and peered under the bed. Several dust bunnies and shoe boxes were there, along with one of her missing slippers, but no book. Starting to feel rather panicky, Olive slid off the bed and rummaged quickly through the room, looking in drawers, under chairs, and inside the closet, where the chalk circle and the bowl of milk stared up at her accusingly. No book.

It had been right beside her last night, she was certain. How could it have just disappeared?

As soon as she'd asked herself this question, Olive knew the answer.

The cats. Of course. They had stolen it from her, slipping in at night to take it right out of her arms, and had craftily hidden it somewhere. *Those stupid, spying, furry little . . .* Fury swept up through Olive's body like the lit fuse of a bottle rocket, burning and hissing upward until: *POW.*

"HORATIO!" Olive shouted, storming out into the hall. "LEOPOLD! HARVEY! GET OUT HERE!"

The empty house absorbed her voice. No one answered. No cats appeared.

Olive thundered down the stairs. A note from her parents hung on the refrigerator, telling her that they had gone to campus and would be back in the late afternoon. White sun, filtered through a screen of shifting leaves, flickered in bright patches on the polished floors. "HORATIO!" Olive yelled again. "HARVEY! LEOPOLD! I KNOW WHAT YOU DID!"

Faster than she'd ever done it before, Olive thumped down the steps into the basement. She yanked the strings of the hanging lightbulbs so hard that they quivered in their sockets. Leopold wasn't in his corner. The trapdoor stood open, just as she had left it. Olive crossed the chilly floor and kicked it shut. Her parents were more likely to notice the trapdoor if it was open . . . probably. Then again, they might not notice unless they fell through it, which wouldn't have a very happy outcome either. Fists on her hips, Olive surveyed the basement. No green eyes flickered at her from the corners.

She stumbled back up the stairs. Her mind beat against the same thought over and over, like a moth throwing itself against a lightbulb: She needed to get the book back. The longer it was missing, the more likely it was that someone else could find it, or that something would happen to it, and she would never see it again. This thought was so awful, Olive had to close her eyes and concentrate on breathing.

If Leopold wasn't in his place, and Horatio was nowhere to be found, there was still one cat to look for, and one other place to check. And Olive finally had a way to get in. She pulled the spectacles out of her pocket and raced up the stairs to the second floor, down the hallway, and into the pink bedroom.

She put on the spectacles with shaking hands. The painting of the stone archway hung before her. Olive extended one hand and felt it slide easily through the warm surface of the painting into the stillness of the attic beyond. She leaned forward, pressing her face through the archway, feeling the painting slide and slip all around her, until she toppled all at once into the dark, dusty alcove. Well, at least she knew the spectacles worked. That was a plus.

She hurried up the stairs, trying to avoid stepping on any dead (or living) wasps with her bare feet.

"Harvey?" she called, reaching the attic floor. "Harvey, I know you can hear me!"

Whether Harvey heard her or not, he didn't answer. Maybe he wasn't in the attic at all. It was hard to imagine the place without Harvey, hiding somewhere in the rafters with his eye patch or his tuna-can breastplate, ready for the next adventure. Olive turned in a slow circle, taking in the dusty jumble of furniture, the silent corners, the shadows where no green eyes glimmered. The room felt stuffy and too quiet . . . and strangely lonely. Olive pulled her mind back to the missing book and let anger shove loneliness aside.

Stalking to the center of the cluttered room, she stripped the covering off of the easel. The pair of painted hands still curved around the scrapbook on the table. Olive could just catch a glimpse of the old photograph on the open page—*Annabelle and Lucinda, aged 14*—but she wasn't about to board that train of thought today. She needed to get the book back.

"Harvey?" Olive called again, unsurprised now when there was no answer.

With a frustrated growl, she stomped toward the round window that overlooked the backyard. There were no cats to be seen in the overgrown garden or darting into the shadows beneath the trees—only a smallish, mussy-haired boy, striding quickly away across Mrs. Nivens's lawn. Peeping around the window's edge, Olive watched Rutherford hurry back into his grandmother's yard. What was he up to? Had he been skulking around her house again, waiting to pester her with more questions about the book? As Olive stared, Rutherford glanced back at the old stone house. Instinctively, she ducked farther into the shadows. But Rutherford didn't seem to see her. A moment later, he had disappeared completely behind the knot of birch trees. Olive breathed a sigh of relief.

Turning back toward the attic, Olive glanced around at the dentist's chair, the mirrors, the miniature cannon, the boxes . . . and the stack of painted canvases. Her mind swirled downward through the house, like a leaf blowing down from the very top of a tree, rushing faster and faster through the hallways, the bedrooms, the main floor, the basement, past the ranks of waiting paintings, and all at once, a sense of how huge and how impossible this search was came over her. The book could be anywhere in this gigantic house—and not just in the house, but Elsewhere. It would take weeks, months, maybe *years* to find it again. If she ever found it at all.

Panic and defeat whirled together in Olive's stomach. She staggered back toward the attic steps, remembering the sensation of being pulled across this floor by invisible strings, and wishing that she felt it now.

Where is the book? Olive asked the house. *Please . . . I need a sign, a clue, anything. Just help me find it.*

The tugging, when it started, was so faint that Olive wasn't sure she felt it at all. She could very well have been imagining it, just like she'd once imagined that she was growing a third eye on her shoulder, which actually turned out to be part of her collarbone (the doctor was very nice about explaining this). She stood at the top of the attic steps, trying to feel which direction the house was pulling her—if it was in fact pulling her at all. She was quite sure that it was pulling her downward, but that might have been gravity. Still, Olive followed the feeling down the attic steps and back through the painting into the pink bedroom.

Once she got there, however, the tugging sensation stopped, leaving her feeling confused and lost and quite a bit heavier than usual. Olive dragged herself along the upstairs hall, looking carefully into the paintings through the spectacles, hoping to see something that sparkled like embossed leather, or a carefully arranged pile of leaves that seemed suspiciously out of place.

She studied the painting of Linden Street, remembering that she could finally climb in on her own again. But she didn't want to. The problem of Morton seemed distant and unpleasant now, like a mass of gray rain clouds on the horizon, which will eventually drift closer and spoil the whole day. The spellbook was much more important. Once she got it back, *maybe* she would think about helping Morton. Maybe.

Olive was still looking so hard at the paintings on the walls that she almost missed what was waiting for her on the floor. (This was especially bad because she had wandered to the top of the staircase, and with one more step she would have sledded down into the foyer face-first.) But at just the right moment, she glanced down and spotted the edge of the first stair . . . and the lilac leaf on the carpet.

Olive halted. Three steps below was another leaf,

and below that, there lay a little cluster of grass clippings, along with a splotch of mud. Olive climbed down the stairs, pulling off the spectacles and putting them into her pocket.

A few crumbs of dirt waited on the hallway floor. Olive crouched down, frowning, and felt a soft, warm breeze ripple over her arms. She glanced up.

The front door of the big stone house was standing open.

17

OLIVE STARED AT the door. It wasn't wide open, but a few inches—just enough that someone could have slipped in or out without making a sound.

She looked over both shoulders, making sure she was alone. Then she darted to the doorway. The porch was empty: no spellbook, no cats, no intruders. Her parents wouldn't have gone out by the front door; they would have gone out the side door, heading toward the garage. And Olive hadn't opened it herself—she hadn't even noticed that it *was* open until just now. She put her hand on the doorknob, looking out onto the shady porch. Was this the sign she'd been asking for?

The porch swing creaked softly on its chains. Baskets of thick ferns nodded in the breeze. Olive shuffled along the floorboards, looking in every corner. Nothing seemed out of place. She trailed down the steps onto the lawn, searching the grass just as she had done only a few days ago, following Harvey's paw prints. So much had happened since then that it felt like years, not days, had passed. A short, sharp ache squeezed Olive's heart. She wished she had something to follow now.

The house loomed over her, its windows dark and empty in the hot midday sun. Olive scanned the front yard—deserted, but for her—and then hurried along the side of the house, toward the back. Remembering the lilac leaf on the stairs, she checked the length of the hedge carefully. Nothing: no book, no broken branches, no telltale scraps of fabric. Olive let out an aggravated breath and turned back toward the yard. The garden looked just as she'd left it—an overgrown tangle of shoots and shrubs. The garden shed leaned crookedly in one corner of the yard. Olive walked toward it, dodging the weedy flowerbeds. She took a deep breath, bracing herself, and tugged open the creaky wooden door.

No one was there.

Olive stepped into the shed, inhaling the smell of moss and soil and rotten wood, glancing up at the old hammock from which she'd rescued Harvey, aka Captain Blackpaw. The memory made her smile, but it was quickly swept away by a new wave of anger.

She couldn't trust the cats anymore. Who did they think they were, anyway? (Well, Harvey thought he was Sir Walter Raleigh, or Lancelot, or Agent 1-800, depending on his mood, but that wasn't really what Olive meant.) This was her house, the cats belonged to the house, and therefore they belonged to her. They were here to do her bidding. How *dare* they refuse to obey her!

Olive halted, startled by her own thoughts. This didn't sound like her. This didn't sound like her at all.

Something outside made a rustling sound. Olive lunged out of the shed and whipped around, inspecting the yard. She stopped beside the compost heap, where she'd buried the painting of the forest with Annabelle McMartin trapped inside it. The ground looked the same as before; here was the slight mound of dirt where she and the cats had filled in the hole. As far as Olive could tell, no one had buried anything else here . . . but just in case, she dropped down onto her knees to take a closer look.

"What are you doing?" said a rapid, slightly nasal voice.

Olive let out a little shriek. She flopped over onto her backside and found herself staring up into the smudgy glasses of Rutherford Dewey. Olive scowled. This was the second time this week that he'd startled her this way, and it had been irritating enough the first time.

"What are *you* doing?" she shot back. "Were you spying on me again?"

"Just because you didn't see me coming doesn't mean I was spying on you," said Rutherford. "I simply walked across your backyard because it provided the quickest route."

"Hmmph," said Olive. "Why are you hanging around my house so much, anyway?"

Rutherford avoided the question. "Was the experiment a success?" he asked, beginning to jiggle enthusiastically from foot to foot. The wrinkled T-shirt he wore today was emblazoned with a picture of two knights jousting, just above the words *Camelot Renaissance Festival: Faire and Balanced.*

Olive scowled at him. "I—" she began, but Rutherford was too excited to let her finish.

"I was thinking about the grimoire itself," he zoomed on. "Obviously, it's quite old, but the fact that it's written in modern English—and I mean *very* modern English, not Shakespeare's version of modern English—means that it definitely postdates the Renaissance, so perhaps it was *translated,* so to speak, by later generations of the family and recopied into a new volume, which would explain—"

"It's gone," said Olive.

Rutherford's words crashed to a stop. He paused, his whole body tilted onto one foot. "The grimoire?"

"I think—" Olive started. "I think it was stolen. It was in my room last night, and when I woke up, it was gone."

"Interesting," said Rutherford. "Do you have any theories about who would have taken it?"

"Almost nobody knew about it, except me. And your grandmother. And *you*." Olive gave Rutherford a close, careful look. He met her eyes, waiting for her to go on.

Olive struggled to her feet, brushing dirt and compost off the seat of her pants. "I think it might have been the cats."

"Oh—like the cat who stole my figurines?" Rutherford started jiggling again. "I suppose that makes sense. Although most common housecats would probably find it difficult to move a large, heavy book."

Olive was tempted to say *They aren't common housecats,* but she stopped herself. "I thought they probably hid it somewhere close by. But then I noticed that the front door was open, and I thought they might have taken it outside."

"I see," said Rutherford. "I could help you look for it."

Olive paused. She took a long look at Rutherford: his messy brown curls, his smudged glasses, his wide-eyed expression. Maybe she *should* let him help. He already knew about the spellbook anyway, the cats were working against her, and Morton hadn't wanted to help her find it in the first place. And, in spite of his straightforward gaze, she still got the feeling that Rutherford knew more about spellbooks than he was telling her. Perhaps if she let him stick around, he would drop a few more hints—and she would be waiting to pick them up.

"Okay," she said slowly. "That's very . . . nice of you."

Rutherford gave her a small bow. "It's part of the code of chivalry, as described by the Duke of Burgundy, to display the virtues of charity, justice, and hope, among other things."

Olive glanced through the shade-spattered yard at the tall stone house, and tried to hear—or feel—what it was telling her. "I don't think it's inside," she said at last. "Let's keep looking out here."

Rutherford gave her another bow and turned toward the cluster of dogwood bushes.

They searched the whole yard, as well as the shed and the garage and the spiderwebby space beneath the porch, but they found nothing. (Well, not quite nothing. Rutherford found something that he thought might be a fragment of a fossil from the cretaceous era, but to Olive it looked more like a bit of broken cement that had had a bottle cap pressed into it.) When they had finished with Olive's yard, they took a brief, sneaky look at Mrs. Nivens's, which didn't take long. Mrs. Nivens's yard was so neat, one out-of-place book would have stood out like a chocolate stain on a wedding dress.

"I don't see anything. Do you?" Olive asked as they leaned side by side into the lilac bushes.

"No. Nothing that seems suspicious." Rutherford pulled back from the bushes and blinked at Olive rapidly behind his smudgy lenses. "What should we try next?"

"I don't know," said Olive. She ripped off a handful of lilac leaves, crushing them in her fist before letting them fall to the ground.

"You should come to my grandmother's house for lunch," said Rutherford. "That way we could formulate a search plan, and we can continue our quest as soon as we're done."

Olive hesitated, chewing on the inside of her lip. Her instinctive answer would have been a quick *no*. She didn't want to have lunch in a strange boy's house, with his nosy grandmother trotting around, listening to everything they said . . . But then again, Rutherford was the only person left who she could talk to about the book. He had been very patient about helping her search—and, as odd as it felt to admit it, even to herself, it was kind of interesting to have him around. She never knew what he was going to say next. Besides, there wasn't anything to eat in her own house except for leftover tuna casserole.

"I guess I could," she said at last. "If you're sure it would be okay with Mrs. Dewey."

"I'm sure. She's always saying I need to take an interest in things that happened within the last six hundred years." Rutherford plunged between the lilac bushes into Mrs. Nivens's backyard. "Let's take the shortcut."

Rutherford walked in a straight, rapid line across Mrs. Nivens's perfect backyard, and Olive followed him more furtively, ducking behind trees or bushes when she could and keeping an eye on Mrs. Nivens's dark windows.

As they wound around the cluster of birch trees, Rutherford kept up a long, rapid-fire lecture about calligraphy before and after the invention of the printing press. Olive wasn't listening. She was looking up at the birches' papery white trunks, trying to see if any traces of green paint remained, and feeling an empty spot in her heart where Harvey used to be. Then the memory of the book flared up, so clear and real that she could almost feel its weight in her arms. Clenching her jaw, Olive turned away from the birch trees and followed Rutherford toward the house.

But they never got there.

". . . For example, stories of King Arthur and the Round Table would have been spread largely by word of mouth, even after Geoffrey of Monmouth began writing them down around 1130, because each copy was handwritten. Then, of course, Thomas Malory's retelling of the legends, published in 1485, became one of the first printed books in England." Rutherford, seeming suddenly to remember that he was talking to another person, turned around to make sure that his audience was listening.

She wasn't. Olive had stopped beside the picnic table. On the table's weathered wooden surface, surrounded by a few flecks of Rutherford's model paint, its embossed leather cover sparkling in the patches of sun that fell through the birch leaves, was the McMartins' book of spells.

Rutherford moved closer to her, craning his head as though trying to get a better look at what lay on the table. It was all Olive could do not to knock him down.

"Is that—" he began.

Olive dove at the table, wrapping the book safely in her arms. "*You* stole it," she hissed.

Rutherford blinked at her. "What?"

"It's mine." Olive took a step backward. "You wanted it for yourself, but you can't have it. It isn't meant for you. It belongs to me."

Rutherford was watching her, his brown eyebrows drawn together. "I didn't take it," he said calmly. "I didn't even know it was here."

"How did it get here, then?" Olive demanded, glaring at him over the edge of the book. "How did it end up in your backyard? Did it get up and walk on its own?"

"I don't know how it got here, but the idea that it moved here on its own doesn't seem very likely."

Olive stomped her foot. "I was being *sarcastic,*" she growled. "And if you didn't take it, and it didn't walk, then how did it get here? Are you saying your grandmother stole it?"

Rutherford tilted his head thoughtfully. "That doesn't seem very likely either, but I don't think we have enough of the facts to draw any sort of conclusion at this point."

"Well, I know one thing," said Olive, pressing the book so hard against her chest that its corners stabbed her in the ribs. "I don't want you in my house, or in my yard, or anywhere near me *ever again.*"

Olive whirled around and ran. She ran across Mrs. Nivens's yard, past her own garden, up the steps of the back porch, and into the cool, quiet shade of the big stone house. Still holding the book tight in one arm, she locked each door and closed every curtain, until the house was as solid as a fortress, where no one could get in or out.

18

FOR THE NEXT few days, Olive didn't leave the house. She didn't even leave her room if she could help it. In the mornings, she burrowed down in bed with the spellbook until her parents left for campus, barely mumbling an answer when her mom and dad called their good-byes through her bedroom door. Then she would run downstairs with the book tucked under her arm, grab whatever fruit or cookies she could carry, and scurry back up to her bedroom.

One morning, as a sort of joke, Mr. Dunwoody slipped a fancy invitation to breakfast under Olive's door. The little card read:

Mr. Alec and Mrs. Alice Dunwoody (aka Dad and Mom) would like the pleasure of Miss Olive Dunwoody's company at the breakfast table at 7:30 a.m. Eggs, toast, fruit, and a selection of beverages to be served. RSUP. (Respond by Showing Up, Please.)

But Olive slept so late that day, she woke up closer to lunch than breakfast. Her parents had left for their office long ago. A plate of very stale toast and very cold eggs was waiting for Olive on the table. She took it with her when she ran back upstairs to study the spellbook again.

While the sun moved from one side of the sky to the other, Olive would lie on her bed, flipping through the pages, and think about attempting another spell. There were several spells that interested her and that didn't sound too difficult. Some were harmless little things—like changing a flower's color from pink to blue—while quite a few others would have ended up with Rutherford running toward a bathroom, making sounds like a whoopee cushion. But every time she came close to trying one, an echo of Horatio's words floated through her brain.

Don't you see what's going on? You're becoming one of them.

And, slowly, Olive would close the book again.

But she never let it out of her sight.

The book sat on the bathroom countertop while she took her bath and brushed her teeth, when she remembered to do these things. (Often, she didn't.) At dinnertime, when her parents called her to the table and Olive couldn't excuse herself without making them suspicious, she would put the book in her backpack and bring it downstairs, setting the bag on the empty chair next to her own, so that it was always within reach.

When her parents noticed this new habit and asked about it—which wasn't until the third evening—Olive explained that she was practicing keeping track of her backpack before school began. The Dunwoodys nodded happily at this. (Olive had lost at least one book bag a year since kindergarten.) Her mind was too full of the spellbook to realize it, but her parents hadn't nodded happily at her in quite a while. Now they gave each other wistful, slightly worried looks as Olive grabbed her backpack, darted away from the table, and thundered up the stairs to her room yet again.

"I suppose it's natural for her to want more privacy," said Mrs. Dunwoody. "She *is* almost a teenager . . ."

"Yes," sighed Mr. Dunwoody. "Only four hundred and thirty-eight days left to go."

Mr. and Mrs. Dunwoody squeezed each other's hands, both of them silently recalling the 4,310 days that the not-quite-teenaged Olive had already been part of their lives.

Meanwhile, behind her closed bedroom door, Olive was squeezing the spellbook tight against her ribs, breathing in its leathery, dusty smell, and wondering how she had ever lived without it.

Each night, she put the book on top of her chest and knotted it in place with a scarf threaded around her body. Then she would tuck the spectacles—which she had also tied to a piece of thick ribbon—into the collar of her pajamas or T-shirt, and close her eyes, with one hand clamped over the spectacles and the other pressed tight to the cover of the book. As Olive quickly discovered, this wasn't the most restful way to sleep. She woke up each morning feeling as though she hadn't slept at all—or as though she had just been through an automatic car wash, but without the car.

Sometimes, while she straightened the spectacles around her neck, Olive thought about visiting Morton, but she always changed her mind before reaching the painting of Linden Street. She still had no answers for him. Mostly what she had for him was anger. Besides, she would have to bring the spellbook Elsewhere with her, to keep it safe, and this meant that Morton would see it, and then Olive would have to explain everything that had happened . . .

And she had enough to worry about as it was.

She could never let her guard down, not even for a second. Strange things were happening around the old stone house, things that made Olive certain that *someone*—or maybe several someones—was still trying to steal the book. Often Olive woke to find her bedroom door open, when she was almost positive that she'd gone to bed with it securely shut. Once, when she hurried downstairs to grab a bag of cookies for breakfast, she found the back door standing ajar.

Finally, when her worries for the book had become so heavy that Olive could hardly climb off of her bed, she decided to take action. There had to be a safe place to keep it—a spot where no one would find it, or even think to look for it. In fact, Olive *knew* there was a spot. She had stood in it, not so long ago, and thought about what an unlikely place it was to hide a secret, special book.

Late one afternoon, when her parents were busy in the library downstairs, Olive put on the backpack with the spellbook zipped securely inside and headed down the hallway to the blue bedroom. She opened the closet and pushed aside the musty wool coats. There, just where she and Morton had left it, was the painting of the crumbling castle. The memory of Morton hit her like a slap on the cheek, but Olive quickly brushed the sting away. Then, with the painting under her arm, she hurried back to her own bedroom.

She laid the painting on the bed. Hershel, her stuffed bear, tipped forward off her pillow, looking down at the canvas interestedly. Olive slid him out of the way before straightening the spectacles on her nose, patting the backpack to make sure the book was still safe inside, and then clambering up onto the mattress and diving down into the painting, as though she were diving through the bed itself.

She landed with a thump on a mossy slope beside the moat. Dark blue sky spread above her, hung with a silver sliver of moon. Its light glanced off of the castle's damp stones and turned the water in the moat into a dim mirror. Olive got to her feet, making her way over the moss toward the drawbridge.

Inside the castle, starlight fell through the open ceiling and over the mottled flagstones of the courtyard. Olive scanned the empty space. Then she crept along the chilly wall, feeling for loose stones, tapping and pushing and prying and pulling until at last a stone rattled under her palm. At the same moment, she thought she heard something else rattle—something that sounded like a pebble clattering across a flagstone floor.

Olive halted, looking over her shoulder. The courtyard was quiet. There was no movement, no sound. What she'd heard was probably just an echo. Turning back toward the wall, Olive tugged at the stone until she felt it give. A gap opened between two slabs, just the right size for hiding the book. While Olive watched, the gap quickly pulled itself shut again. Her heart gave a little leap. This was the perfect spot. Olive was just about to open her backpack when a flicker of light reached over her shoulder.

She spun around, flattening herself against the wall. Someone was approaching.

With the light in her eyes, she could make out nothing more than a silhouette hurrying through one of the stone archways in the walls, but even from this distance she could see that it was a person—a largish, stocky person, holding up an old-fashioned lantern. The light from the lantern made a rippling pool of pale color that glided across the stones.

"Who goes there?" shouted the silhouette, coming closer.

"Um . . . it's . . . it's Olive," squeaked Olive, pressing herself against the wall like a squashed fly.

As it came nearer, the silhouette turned into a man: a shaggy, rather dirty man, bundled up in layers of gray cloaks, with a wide, friendly face. He raised the lantern and peered at Olive. "Oh," he said in surprise. "You're the little girl. I thought you might be the lady who came before."

Olive bristled slightly at being called "a little girl," but she decided that this was not the time to make an issue of it. "No," she said, swinging the backpack over her shoulder again. "The lady who used to live here died. Now it's just my parents and me."

The scruffy man stared at her interestedly. Could he possibly have guessed what she was doing? Olive couldn't be certain. But she *was* certain that she

couldn't hide the book here now—not with this nosy man nearby.

"I was just—looking for something," Olive mumbled, frustrated, beginning to back away. "But I don't think it's here. I guess I'll have to look someplace else."

"Perhaps I can help you find it," the man offered, before Olive could dodge away. "I'm the porter. It's my job to let people in and out of the castle, answer questions, show people around and such. But, of course, there hasn't been anyone to show around. Not for quite a while. Well . . ." He hesitated. ". . . That is, there was someone to show around. But I didn't do it. I just kept an eye on them."

"Them?" repeated Olive, sidling toward the doorway.

"*You,* that is. And the little boy in his nightclothes."

Olive stopped sidling. She looked at the porter, waiting for him to go on.

He brushed a smudge of soot across his nose. "I hid, and I watched you," he said a bit bashfully as the soot rearranged itself into its original shape. "At first, I thought you might have been the lady, or maybe you were her spies. She told me if I ever spoke to anyone again, she would come back and"—the porter swallowed hard—"get rid of me for good."

"Yeah, that sounds like the lady who used to live

here," said Olive, backing toward the doorway again. Inside her backpack, the spellbook was growing heavier.

"But that's a porter's *job,*" the man insisted, as though Olive had said it wasn't. "Would you like me to show you around?" he asked eagerly. "You could go back out and cross the drawbridge again, and this time, I could stand at the other end and hold up the lantern, so you could see your way in."

"Thanks, but I really have to be going." Olive turned and lunged through the arch.

"I'm sorry that I thought you were the lady," the porter went on, trailing after Olive like a large, dirty puppy. "You don't actually look like her at all."

"Oh," said Olive, wincing. The spellbook had grown so heavy that the straps of her backpack dug into her shoulders. She had to get out of here so she could set the book down someplace safe.

"First of all, she was a good bit older than you are. Thirty, forty years, I'd say. And she was wearing a dress. And she was real neat; not a hair out of place. And *she* wasn't in such a hurry to leave again," he added in a put-off tone, breaking into a trot to keep up with Olive. "She sat right down and stayed. She said she'd found this castle waiting to be hung up, and she'd hidden it someplace where it wouldn't be disturbed. She had a pair of spectacles on her—gold ones, on a chain, sort of like those ones you've got. She said she'd stolen them from her friend, but she was going to give them back, so it was really no more than borrowing. And she said she would stay here as long as it took for her to change, because her friend certainly wasn't going to do it for her."

Olive, who had been teetering carefully across the drawbridge, whirled around and nearly lost her balance. The porter stood on the other end of the drawbridge, holding up the lantern. She stared at his bristly face in the dim light. He couldn't be talking about Annabelle McMartin; she wouldn't have *stolen* the spectacles . . .

"What did the lady say?" Olive breathed.

"She said she'd stay as long as it took for her to change," the porter repeated. "That her friend wasn't going to do it for her, even though she had promised that they would be together forever, part of the same family."

"Until she changed . . . into paint?"

The porter shrugged. The lantern swung in his hand, sending its dim beams across the moat. Then his eyebrows went up and his face took on a look of surprise, as though a long-lost memory had just popped up in his brain. "She said . . ." He paused, thinking. "She said her friend had changed her mind about making her the heir, whatever that means. But now, she said, one day her friend would die, and *she* wouldn't." The porter shrugged again. "She stayed a long time. Had a nice visit. Until she threatened me, that is." He glanced down at the silvery water. "It was good to have someone to talk to. It's dull work being a porter when there's never anyone at your door."

Olive wavered at the end of the drawbridge. The weight of the spellbook pulled against her shoulders, gouging into her skin. She could feel the house tugging at her too, guiding her back toward the painting's edge, where the glinting frame hung in the cool blue air.

"This lady—did she say what her name was?" she asked, backing slowly toward the frame.

The porter pursed his lips and tilted his head, "It was Mrs. . . . something-or-other. Think it started with an M or an N. But I remember that *Mrs.* bit, because I said, 'Oh, so you're married?' trying to be polite, and she said, 'No,' sort of sour-like. 'I never was, and now I never will be. But people stopped calling me *miss* a long time ago.'"

Inside the backpack, the book seemed to be growing even heavier. Dazed, feeling as though she was being dragged backward, Olive stumbled toward the edge of the painting.

"Well, good-bye, then," called the porter, sounding a bit miffed.

"Bye," answered Olive. She arranged the spectacles on her nose.

"You can come back and visit anytime, you know—"

But Olive was already halfway out of the painting, crawling onto her springy mattress. Once she was all the way out, she kicked the castle painting to the floor, so that she could sprawl full length over the blankets and try to think. But every time she tried to put the pieces together, the spellbook popped up instead, scattering all her other thoughts as lightly as particles of dust.

With an aggravated sigh, Olive unzipped the backpack and took out the book. It weighed just as much as it always had—it was thick and solid, but not difficult to lift. And it was very easy to hold it up and squeeze it against her ribs with both arms. Obviously, the spellbook didn't want to be away from her. It didn't want to be left alone in a painting. And who could blame it? Morton certainly complained enough about it . . .

Morton. Olive wriggled out of a loop of guilty thoughts. Why should she worry so much about helping Morton, anyway? He was just a painting. He was where he belonged. And she had much better things to think about—things like this book, which *wasn't* a painting, which belonged out here in the real world, with her.

Olive rolled onto her back, wrapping the spellbook tightly in her arms. She imagined that it was holding her, as well—that delicate silver threads or roots were branching off of its leather cover, wrapping around her ribs, around her heart, until she and the book were one.

THAT NIGHT, OLIVE dreamt of the tree again. Somehow it seemed even bigger than before, its blue branches sparkling with silver starlight, its leaves whispering like a chorus of a thousand voices. *Olive,* they whispered. *Olive . . . Olive . . .*

Standing on the dewy grass, Olive leaned back, looking up and up and up. The tree seemed to reach for her, beckoning to her. It blocked out the sky. It held out its open arms.

Olive had never been much of a tree-climber. Anyone who frequently falls over her own toes isn't likely to risk falling from anything higher than a bed (and Olive had fallen out of bed enough times to be a bit wary of *that*), but climbing this tree hardly felt like climbing at all. As soon as she had shimmied up the trunk to the first branches, she felt as though she were being pulled along, hoisted up by invisible hands. Maybe the branches themselves were helping her. She was weightless and graceful. She floated like milkweed. Dewy breezes played with the ends of her hair.

As she climbed through the whispering blue leaves, Olive noticed something sparkling on the tree limbs—something she originally thought was just a trace of starlight flaring on the glossy bark. As her hands clasped one smooth, stone-solid branch, the sparkling outline flared to life. Floating just above her fingers was a row of glittering letters. Olive read them. *Athdar McMartin.*

She climbed higher. Another name glistened beside her, sparkling like dragonflies' wings: *Ansley McMartin.* She climbed past *Alastair McMartin* and *Angus McMartin,* and *Ailsa* and *Aillil* and *Argyle McMartin.* The names dimmed again as she left them behind. She was getting close to something wonderful; she could feel it.

Even at the highest reaches of the tree, the branches felt strong and solid. The leaves thickened, forming a rippling, whispering dome. *Olive . . . Olive . . .* they called. And Olive climbed.

Aldous McMartin flared and burned out as she left his branch behind. There was *Annabelle McMartin,* the delicate chain of silver letters beckoning her to the highest branch. And finally, Olive had reached the top of the tree. Above her fists, the final name glistened. *Olive Dunwoody*. Olive pulled herself onto the last branch, and slowly, fearlessly, she stood up. Her head broke through the canopy of leaves, and the whole tall blue tree rustled and sparkled below her. She could see to the ends of the earth. The ground glimmered far below her. The sky above was purple and rich with stars. She took a deep breath.

Olive. Olive. Olive . . .

If she jumped now, she would fly. She would soar like a snowy owl, or drift on the breezes, like a cottonwood seed. The voices would hold her up. They wouldn't let her fall.

Olive curved her toes over the edge of the branch and spread her arms. The air was sweet and cool, billowing around her, tugging eagerly at her cotton pajamas. She closed her eyes.

Jump, Olive, said the thousand whispering voices. *Jump. Jump.*

Olive bent her knees. She took a last, deep breath—

Something sharp tore into her ankle.

Olive's eyes flicked open. The tree vanished as suddenly as if it had been pounded into the earth like a big, leafy nail. By the silver-blue light of a distant streetlamp, she could make out the pattern on her penguin pajamas.

Below the pajamas were her own bare feet. Just beyond her bare feet, the edge of the roof of the old stone house glinted dimly, and, between the pajamas and the feet, a huge black cat was biting her leg.

Olive let out a gasp and staggered back from the edge.

The cat looked up. "I'm sorry, miss. Did I hurt you?"

"No . . ." choked Olive. "Not really."

"Oh," said Leopold, with just a hint of disappointment. "Well. Good."

Olive took a dizzy look around. She was standing at the highest point of the roof, just above the attic's peaked ceiling. Far, far below, the backyard with its overgrown gardens rustled softly. One far-off streetlamp sent its glow across the yard, dipping everything in dull silver. Just a few inches in front of her toes, the roof ended, severed by the darkness.

"How did I get up here?" Olive whispered to the cat.

"You climbed."

"I *climbed*?" Olive breathed. She edged forward, craning to see over the ledge. It was a very long way down.

"It was most impressive," said Leopold. "You climbed onto the porch roof, up the drainpipe, onto a window ledge, and over the edge of the roof."

Olive's knees, frightened by the view, suddenly decided to go on strike. She plunked down on her backside, grasping the shingles with both hands, while Leopold's green eyes scanned the darkness.

"How did you find me?" she asked, when she could get her brain and lungs and mouth all working together again.

"I didn't find you," said Leopold stiffly. "I followed you. I've been following you on all of your nightly expeditions. This is the farthest afield you've ever gone, except for the night when you left the book on Mrs. Dewey's picnic table, but—"

"Wait—*what*?" Olive interrupted, her mind reeling. "When *I* left the book there? You mean I've done this before?"

"You've done this almost every night since you found that . . . that *book*." Here the big cat paused for a second, swallowing what sounded suspiciously like a lump in his throat.

"But, Leopold," said Olive, rapidly scraping her thoughts back together, "I don't walk in my sleep!"

"I can assure you that you do, miss. Of course, you might not have realized it, because you are generally asleep at the time," Leopold explained, nodding his head wisely. "It's a bit like when someone insists she doesn't snore, because she's never awake to hear the snoring."

"You mean . . ." Olive began. "But I *don't* snore!"

Leopold gave her a long, significant look.

Olive pulled her knees close to her chest. The night was chilly. The whole world had turned gray in the darkness: the grass, the trees, her own hands. Only Leopold's eyes kept their bright green color.

"You didn't give up on me," Olive whispered. "You followed me, just in case. You stopped me before I really got hurt. You were still trying to help me, even though I did something awful to you." A choking feeling squeezed her throat, but Olive struggled on. "Thank you, Leopold."

Leopold looked a bit embarrassed. He blinked and glanced away, pretending to scan the sky until he could get his face back under strict control. Then he patted Olive's foot with his soft black paw. "There, there, miss," he said gruffly.

Olive wiped her face on her sleeve and snuffled.

"Well," said Leopold, making up for this show of emotion by puffing out his chest even farther than usual, "we should get you back to safety. Hup to it." He got to his feet with a little swagger. "Follow me, miss. We'll climb in through a window, and I'll have you down in no time."

Feeling very wobbly and jelly-kneed, Olive stood up. But she hadn't taken a single step before something glinting in the darkness far below caught her eye. She stopped, looking hard.

On the ground, near the garden shed, a shovel was standing straight up in a mound of dirt. Its metal handle shone in the light from the streetlamp. Beside the shovel was a hole, its empty mouth filled with shadows.

Olive's knees locked. She staggered, catching herself just in time to keep from toppling over the edge of the roof.

"Leopold," she choked, "who dug up the painting?"

Leopold looked back at her, his green eyes wide and bright in the darkness. "Why, *you* did, miss."

20

"But I don't remember digging up *anything!*" Olive cried.

They were standing beside the hole in the backyard, having slipped in through an upstairs window and raced down through the sleeping house. Just as Olive had already known it would be, the forest painting—with Annabelle trapped inside it—was gone.

"Keep your voice low, miss," said Leopold, glancing around.

"What did I do with it after I dug it up?" Olive whispered desperately. "Did you see?"

Leopold gave his head a short shake. "Negative, I'm afraid. I was watching through a window, and I only got there in time to see you pull up the painting and vanish through the lilac hedge. By the time I got out-doors, you had disappeared."

Olive plunked to the ground and hid her face in her arms. "Oh, Leopold . . ." she moaned. The pieces were falling into place, and Olive did not like the picture they formed. The search for the book had made her fight with Morton. The book had made her hurt the cats, and forced them to turn against her. It had made her avoid her parents. It had come between her and Rutherford. It had caused her to walk in her sleep, dig up the painting, and leave it who-knows-where. If Leopold hadn't stopped her, it would have guided her right over the edge of the roof.

It had tricked her, trying to make her believe that she belonged there, that she could use the magic in its pages, that she could be one of the McMartins and still be herself.

And, with this realization, the silvery mist in Olive's mind burned away. Beneath it was the truth. It had been there all along. The book, like the house, was trying to get rid of her. And once Olive was out of the way, it would be very easy to bring someone else *back*. All it would take was . . .

Olive clutched at the front of her pajamas. The spectacles were gone.

She let out a little shriek.

"Shh!" hissed Leopold, moving into a crouch.

Olive froze.

A low crackling noise drifted out of the shadows nearby, then stopped. Olive and Leopold waited, scanning the canopy of trees that spread thickly above them.

"Perhaps it was just a squirrel," said Leopold.

Snap. A twig broke, sending its sharp report out through the night.

"Are squirrels nocturnal?" Olive squeaked.

Leopold didn't answer. He gave the trees a long, squinty look. "Don't be alarmed, miss," he whispered, positioning himself protectively in front of her, "but I believe we're being watched."

Olive's heart leaped into high gear. "I'm not sure there's anything more alarming than the words 'Don't be alarmed,'" she whispered back, wriggling even closer to the cat. Leopold didn't answer. His bright green eyes tilted slowly upward.

A sudden, wild rustling came from the branches just above Olive's head. Olive froze, holding her breath. Leopold hissed. There was the loud crack of a branch breaking, followed by a muffled yowl, and then a ball of tree limbs and multicolored fur was plummeting toward the ground in front of them. At the last minute, it flipped itself over, landing on all fours in a small explosion of leaves and fresh black paint.

Olive and Leopold leaned closer. In the middle of a pile of leafy detritus, a cat crouched on the ground.

From beneath a black trickle of paint and a lopsided beret of leaves, his wild green eyes ricocheted from Olive to Leopold and back again.

"Harvey!" Olive exclaimed.

The cat's wide eyes grew even wider. "You didn't see me!" he screeched. Then he bolted away toward the lilac hedge.

Olive and Leopold stood still for a few moments, staring after the rapidly vanishing cat.

"Is he being a spy, or is he still mad at me?" Olive asked at last.

Leopold tilted his head to one side. "It's hard to say," he answered slowly. "You never really know with Harvey."

"Is . . ." Olive began, finding the question harder to get out than she had expected. ". . . Is Horatio still mad at me?"

"Oh-HO, yes," said Leopold.

"Leopold," said Olive as the feeling of horror that had been briefly brushed away settled over her again, "the spectacles are gone too."

Leopold's eyes darted to her face.

"If the same person who has the painting also has the spectacles . . ." Olive couldn't go on. The next words were too horrible. She had wasted her chance to let Morton out of his painting, even temporarily. Now whoever had the spectacles could let out *someone else*.

Olive closed her eyes and tried to think. Maybe it was because she was far away from the book, or maybe it was because the house had already gotten what it wanted from her, but suddenly all the threads of ideas in Olive's mind rearranged themselves into a strong, sparkling web. She thought of the photograph of Morton and his family, and of the familiar face of the neat, chilly-looking girl. She thought of the same girl in the scrapbook up in the attic, in the picture labeled *Annabelle and Lucinda, aged 14*. She thought about the strange skin of Mrs. Nivens's hand. She thought of what the porter in the painting had said, about the cold, tidy woman who had climbed inside and waited and waited . . .

Olive's whole body jerked as though she'd gotten an electric shock. She whirled away from the painting's empty hole and raced toward the hedge.

"Miss!" hissed Leopold, bounding after her. "What are you doing?"

"I think I know who has them," Olive hissed back over her shoulder. She was already pushing apart the lilac branches when something to her right gave a loud rustle.

"Psst," said a voice from the bushes.

Together, Leopold and Olive slunk closer. A soft crinkling sound came from within the hedge, and as Leopold and Olive stared, a messy, black-streaked ball crept toward them, its bright green eyes wide with excitement.

"Are we alone?" the ball whispered in a faint British accent.

"Negative," answered Leopold, as though this was obvious. "We're together."

"It's me—Agent 1-800," the ball hissed. "I have information. *Valuable* information. I've been slipping back and forth through enemy lines like a thumb in a game of cat's cradle. I've been gathering secrets like a gardener in a danger-patch. I've been—"

"Oh, Agent 1-800," said Olive, sprawling flat on her stomach to get closer to the cat's paint-streaked face, "I have really missed you."

Harvey looked at her for a moment. Something in his eyes softened slightly. "I was never far away," he said with a jaunty toss of his head. Several ferns, stuck to the black paint above his ear, also tossed jauntily. "I've been watching you all along. You never even knew I was there."

"Well," objected Olive, "just a few minutes ago, when you—"

"Exactly!" Harvey crowed obliviously. "You never had any idea. That's why they call me the greatest spy of them all!"

"I thought they called you Agent 1-800," said Leopold.

"They call me *both*," said Harvey, starting to look testy, "because I'm . . ." Here he broke off, glaring from one of them to the other. "See here, do you want this information or not?"

"We do," said Olive quickly.

Harvey gave a solemn nod. "Here it is, then. Top secret. Highly classified. For your ears only. Signed, sealed, and delivered. Prepackaged for your convenience. Understood?"

Leopold only looked confused, but Olive nodded hard enough for both of them.

"The bread is in the breadbox," Harvey whispered, his eyes bright pinpoints in the darkness. "If you get my drift."

"I don't," said Olive.

"The pickle is in the jar." He stared at Olive, waiting for a sign of comprehension. "The bat is in the cave. The wax is in the ear."

Olive was tempted, not for the first time, to grab Harvey and see if she could shake something that made sense out of him. "Do you mean, *the painting is in Mrs. Nivens's house?*"

Harvey let an aggravated breath out through his nose. Then, grudgingly, he gave a small nod.

Olive leaped to her feet and thrust the lilac bushes apart. "I knew it. I'm going to get it back."

"Miss!" Leopold protested. "It's too dangerous!"

"Proceed with caution, Agent Olive!" Harvey slunk through the trunks of the lilac bushes, his eyes honed on Olive as she ventured onto the grass.

A faint tinge of blue light was beginning to creep up from the horizon, giving Mrs. Nivens's gray house a ghostly glow, but there was at least an hour before dawn. Olive scanned the windows, but she couldn't see anything through the glass—no movement, no chilly face staring back out. Crouching low, Olive slunk past the neat beds of roses. Their thorns snagged on her pajamas.

Hopping over a petunia border, she pressed her back against the side of the tall gray house, where she couldn't be seen from the street or through the windows. Olive spread her arms, flattening herself tight to the wall. She tried to imagine herself sliding across the wooden clapboard as placidly as a starfish, but her hands were shaking and her knees wobbled, and her breath came out of her nose in whiffling little puffs.

A rock suddenly rolled beneath her bare foot, dragging Olive's leg out from under her. She wobbled and caught herself before she could fall over backward, but the click of the rock reverberated in her head like a gunshot. A few moments passed with Olive pressed against the side of the house, rattling with adrenaline. With a delicate, tiptoeing step, Olive edged beneath the side windows. Then she turned and inched her way up until her nose was level with the window ledge.

In the dim light, Olive could just make out the interior of Mrs. Nivens's living room. Everything in the room was white: white carpet, white couch, white lace doilies everywhere, just waiting for someone to bumble along and stain them. But other than the whiteness, there was nothing odd about this room. There were no books, as far as Olive could see. The objects displayed in shiny glass cases looked a lot more breakable than interesting: little porcelain dolls with droopy eyes, crystal eggs, miniature vases without flowers. Mrs. Nivens wasn't there. And there were no paintings or spectacles to be seen. But coming from somewhere on the other side of the house, perhaps slipping through the gap beneath a closed door, was a thin golden trickle of light.

Olive dropped back down, half crouching, half crawling around to the other side of Mrs. Nivens's house.

"Miss!" hissed Leopold's voice from a nearby rose-bush.

"Agent Olive, what are you doing?" whispered Harvey, blinking out at her from the thorny branches.

"Stay there and keep watch," Olive whispered back. "If I don't come back in ten minutes . . ." She glanced up at the towering gray house. "I don't know. But I have to get the spectacles."

"Come back, miss!" Leopold called. But Olive was already darting around the corner.

She had to wriggle behind a row of hydrangeas to get close to these windows. As she crouched there, panting a little, she listened for footsteps or squeaking doors, but the tall wooden house was quiet. Olive wrapped her fingers over the sill and pulled herself up onto her tiptoes.

The curtains in this room were closed. Through the tiny, half-inch gap between them, Olive could see a band of golden light. Someone inside the room moved, and a rippling shadow passed over the curtains, but Olive couldn't tell who the shadow belonged to, whether it was Mrs. Nivens, or . . . someone else.

Think, she told herself. *If you're right, and you do see Mrs. Nivens with the spectacles, or the painting, or even* (she had to swallow hard) *Annabelle McMartin, what are you going to do about it?*

Well, she answered herself, *I'm going to stay hidden. First, I'll steal the spectacles back without them seeing me. If I'm lucky, and Annabelle's still in the painting, then I'll steal that back too. And if Annabelle isn't in the painting . . .*

Olive shook her head. She'd deal with that possibility if she had to. The important thing was not to be seen. Annabelle had already tried to kill her once, and that was *before* Olive had destroyed the last existing image of Annabelle's grandfather and buried Annabelle under a pile of compost. If Mrs. Nivens and Ms. McMartin—or *Lucinda and Annabelle*—saw her, there was no telling what they would do.

Cautiously, quietly, Olive pulled herself higher and pressed her nose against the pane. She was so intent on watching the inside of the room that she couldn't see or hear anything outside of it. She didn't hear the soft steps on the grass, or the gentle rustling of the hydrangea leaves. She didn't notice that she was no longer alone until a cool, smooth hand had wrapped itself firmly around her wrist.

"COME WITH ME, *right now*," Mrs. Dewey said into Olive's ear. Her voice was soft, but something in it managed to knock every argument out of Olive's head.

Holding tight to Olive's wrist, Mrs. Dewey turned and marched away from Mrs. Nivens's house so quickly that Olive had to jog to keep up. She stumbled behind Mrs. Dewey's wide, bathrobe-swaddled backside across the dark lawns, around a clump of trees, and up to the front door of Mrs. Dewey's house.

Olive had never been inside Mrs. Dewey's house before. Now she was too terrified to take a good look around, and besides, Mrs. Dewey was still dragging her along at such a fast pace that all Olive could see was a blur of leaves and flowers and green fronds uncurling from pots on every surface.

Mrs. Dewey plunked Olive down at the kitchen table and began making clattering noises on the stove. Olive sat in a daze, staring at the yellow checkered tablecloth, and wondered if Mrs. Dewey was getting ready to eat her. It was Olive's understanding, thanks to many books of fairy tales, that this often happened to nosy children. And Mrs. Dewey ate large portions of *something,* that was for sure.

Or maybe Mrs. Dewey had an even worse punishment in mind. Yes . . . at any minute, she might pick up the phone and tell Mrs. Nivens, "Do you know what that weird little girl from next door was doing *now*? Would you like to come over here and deal with her yourself?"

Olive's mind wanted to make a break for it—hop up from the table, bolt out the front door, and run until it was safe underneath her own bed. Her body, on the other hand, was determined not to do anything. Every muscle had turned to terrified jelly. Even her bones felt floppy. Olive had learned from a nature documentary that some frightened animals do amazing things to save themselves. They squirt ink, or give off a terrible smell, or puff up into a spiky basketball twenty times their usual size, while other animals—opossums and similar slow, furry creatures—play dead. Olive fell into the opossum category.

She had slumped so far into her chair by the time

Mrs. Dewey set a cup in front of her that she almost knocked the cup over with her nose.

"It's only cocoa," Mrs. Dewey said when Olive looked up in surprise. "And I made some for you too, so you might as well come in here," she snapped toward the doorway, where one lens of Rutherford's smudged glasses was peering not-very-sneakily into the room.

Rutherford, in a set of extremely wrinkled pajamas, sidled across the kitchen to pour his own cocoa. His curly brown hair, which was even more mussed and rumpled than usual, stood up on his head like some large, asymmetrical sea creature. He sat down beside Olive at the kitchen table. They exchanged a short, shy glance.

Mrs. Dewey sighed, settling herself across from Olive with a flowery pink cup and saucer. "I know what you're about to do, Olive," she began. "But listen to what I tell you. *You need to be careful.* Don't go any-where near Mrs. Nivens's house unless you absolutely have to. And if you have to . . ." She paused. ". . . then be prepared." Her eyes swiveled to Rutherford. "That goes for you too, Sir Talks-A-Lot."

Olive gulped, still too jelly-like to move. "Why?" she croaked.

"I think you already know why." Mrs. Dewey gave her a significant look, tapped her tiny teaspoon against the rim of the cup, and took a delicate sip. "Do you know why I moved to this house?" she asked, after a short pause. "This *particular* house, on this *particular* street?"

Olive shrugged.

"Reasonable mortgage rates?" asked Rutherford. Both Mrs. Dewey and Olive stared at him for a moment.

"No," said Mrs. Dewey. "It was because of the McMartins, and by extension, because of Mrs. Nivens. I'm here to keep an eye on them."

"You mean . . . you really *are* a spy?" whispered Olive, wondering if for once Harvey had gotten the facts straight.

Mrs. Dewey pursed her little pink mouth. "Not exactly." She glanced down at the cup in front of Olive. "You're not drinking your cocoa, Olive. Would you like some whipped cream? Or some marshmallows?"

"No, that's . . ."

But Mrs. Dewey was already up, tottering around the kitchen in her little high heels. "I'm sure I have some marshmallows here." After some time rustling through the stuffed cupboards, Mrs. Dewey found a bag of marshmallows and set them on the table. To be polite, Olive took a handful of them, dropped them into her cocoa, and swallowed several of them whole when she took her first gulp.

"I have something else for you," said Mrs. Dewey. Olive looked up. Mrs. Dewey was holding a tiny canvas bag, barely large enough for a set of jacks. She took the lid off of a flowery ceramic cookie jar, removed one pale yellow macaroon, and placed it inside the bag.

"Am I supposed to save that for later?" asked Olive, confused.

"It's not to eat," said Mrs. Dewey. "Rutherford, why don't you go get the figurine you painted for Olive?"

Rutherford hesitated for a moment, staring hard at Olive from behind his slightly crooked glasses. Then he glanced at his grandmother, who gave him a little prompting nod. Slowly—more slowly than Olive had ever seen him move—Rutherford got up and left the kitchen. He returned a minute later with a tiny, painted metal knight on horseback. He held it out on his palm so that Olive could get a closer look. "That's a French coat of arms on the shield," he said, looking at the figurine, not at Olive. "It dates back to the knights at Agincourt."

Olive examined the tiny symbols. Every strand of hair on the little metal horse and every detail of the knight's armor had been colored with strokes as thin as spider's thread. "It's really nice," she said softly, trying to look into Rutherford's eyes, but only getting as far as his chin.

"You're welcome," said Rutherford, even though Olive hadn't said "thank you." Then he handed the figurine to his grandmother, who slipped it into the canvas bag.

Mrs. Dewey pulled the bag's drawstring, which was long enough that she could easily slip it over Olive's head. "There," she said, straightening the little bag. "For protection."

"A cookie and a model knight?" Olive asked doubtfully, tucking the little bag inside the collar of her pajamas.

Mrs. Dewey's eyes flicked down to hers. For the first time, Olive noticed what a bright shade of blue they were. "Two gifts, made with care and good wishes, just for you," she said firmly. "Not all magic is dark, you know." She gave Olive a little smile and then carried her cup and saucer to the sink. "But it won't last forever. Three or four days, tops," she added, with a glance out the kitchen window. "The sun is coming up. You'll be safe outside now. Hurry home before your parents worry."

Rutherford walked Olive to the door. Olive hesitated on the stoop for a moment, looking out over Linden Street. The sky had turned a pale, watery blue, and the first faint rays of sunlight landed on the sleepy houses, glinting on green leaves and dewy flowers. Even Mrs. Nivens's house looked peaceful. The light that had been burning downstairs had gone out.

Olive gave Rutherford a long look out of the corner of her eye. "Now I think I understand how you knew about grimoires."

Rutherford glanced back at her, looking almost—but not quite—sheepish. "My grandmother won't even let me look at hers," he said. "She says she won't start teaching me until I'm considerably older, because improper use of magic can be too dangerous, and because my parents would have a bird. Those are *her* words," he added quickly. "I would never suggest that a human being would give birth to a bird, or lay an egg containing a bird, as the case may be."

"Then when she saw us in my garden with the spell-book, why didn't she stop us?"

Rutherford shrugged. "She wanted me to keep an eye on you, so to speak. I was supposed to find out what you were doing with the grimoire and try to determine whose side you were on before Grandmother told you anything about us."

Olive folded her arms. "So you *have* been spying on me!"

"I wasn't *spying*," Rutherford argued. "I was just supposed to monitor you, as it were. And protect you, if I could."

"And that's why you've been hanging around my house so much?" said Olive, feeling slightly hurt, and then feeling surprised by her feelings.

"That's part of it." Rutherford tilted his head. "But you know how every object has a gravitational pull related to its mass?"

"...Kind of."

"Your house has a gravitational pull much stronger than its mass would suggest."

"I know what you mean." Olive paused, looking up the street toward the looming rooftop of the old stone house. "Rutherford—I—I think I'm going to need your help doing something very important. But first...I have to explain some things to you. Things about my house. They're going to sound weird and hard to believe—"

But Olive didn't get any further. At that moment, one large black cat and one smaller cat covered in a patchy coat of black paint rushed out of the shadows toward the stoop.

"Agent Olive!" Harvey exclaimed, not noticing Rutherford standing beside her. "Are you all—"

Leopold clamped a paw over Harvey's mouth.

Rutherford's eyes widened.

Olive took a deep breath. "They're going to sound weird and hard to believe," she repeated, "but I swear, they're all true."

SEVERAL MINUTES LATER, a very tired and droopy Olive Dunwoody walked back up the sidewalk to her own house. Leopold and Harvey trotted beside her, both of them casting frequent distrustful looks at Mrs. Nivens's silent house next door.

Mr. Dunwoody was standing on the porch of the big stone house, already dressed for the day, sipping what was obviously his sixth or seventh cup of coffee and beaming delightedly out at the quiet street. The cats bolted past him through the open front door. Mr. Dunwoody gave them a cheery nod.

"Olive!" he called out as she tromped up the steps onto the porch in her bedraggled, pajamas. "I see you've been out enjoying the fresh air. Isn't it a glorious morning?"

Olive gave a wan little smile. She sidled carefully past her father, who had gone back to sighing and beaming at the morning sun, slipped through the door, and climbed the stairs to her bedroom.

The spellbook lay on her bed, its leather cover sparkling amid the rumpled blankets. Now the sparkling didn't seem enticing to Olive. Now it seemed malicious, like the glint in someone's eye before he pelts you with a spitball. Olive turned away.

First, she changed into a clean set of clothes, picking out her darkest pants and shirt. She tucked the little bag from Mrs. Dewey carefully down her collar, where it scratched lightly against her skin. Then she took a piece of paper and a pen out of her art supply drawer and sat down on the edge of the bed to write.

"Horatio," she read aloud, "I don't know if you're nearby, or if you can hear me, or if you're even listening to anything I say anymore. That's why I'm writing this note too, just in case. I should have believed you about the book. I should have listened to you. I'm sorry I ever used it. I don't want to be like *THEM,* and I know the book is theirs, not mine, and it isn't good for me. So I want you to put it away somewhere. Hide it so no one can find it, not even me. Because I trust you. I really, really do. Love, Olive."

Olive folded the note in half and wrote *Horatio* on the outside. She left it on top of the book's sparkling leather cover. Then she stepped out into the hallway and closed the door firmly behind her.

Olive, Leopold, and Harvey (who was still covered in black paint and quite a lot of sticky leaves, because there were more important matters at hand than cat baths) stood together at the bottom of the hill inside the painting of Linden Street. Olive was dreading this next step, but she knew there was no way around it. She owed it to Morton.

One more time, she checked that the photograph of Lucinda and Annabelle was still safe in her pocket. Harvey had been more than delighted to retrieve the photo from the scrapbook between the disembodied hands in the attic, once Olive had explained that it was a top-secret, type-A, sealed file, required to bring down an internal ring of spies.

"Come on, Agent Olive!" Harvey called over his shoulder, taking off toward the street. "Time is of the essence!"

Leopold gave her a reassuring nod, and together they hurried up the misty hill toward the row of houses.

As they approached the tall gray house, a familiar voice trailed toward them across the twilit lawn. The cats crouched behind a little roll in the turf, peeping over the edge.

"Ready . . . set . . . go!" There was a muffled *thwump*. "I win again!"

Olive could hear the rustling of Morton's big cotton nightshirt before she even caught a glimpse of him. He was racing toward his house, climbing up the steps, hopping onto the porch rail, and hoisting himself from there onto the porch's roof.

"Ready . . ." he yelled, backing up toward the inner edge of the roof. "Set . . ."

"Morton, NO!" shouted Olive.

Morton teetered, glancing around until he caught sight of Olive staring up at him. "Why did you stop me?" He flapped his arms angrily. "That one was a draw, Elmer. It doesn't count," he said, turning toward another spot on the ground. "I know. She always ruins things." He shot Olive a glare.

"I just don't want you to hurt yourself," said Olive, trying to hold on to her patience, which, in Morton's presence, often behaved like a slippery fish.

"Watch me," said Morton. Then he ran off the edge of the porch roof.

Involuntarily, Olive let out a squeak. Morton landed with a *thump* on both feet and turned to her with a smug little smile. "Told you," he said. "I jumped from the very top before, and it didn't even hurt. Well, it *hurt,* but then the hurt went away. See?" He pulled up the hem of his nightshirt, showing Olive his lower leg. "The bone went all funny, but then it snapped back again. I didn't even get any bruises."

Olive squinted through the twilight at Morton's shin. "You mean your leg broke, and then it healed?"

"I guess so," said Morton.

"I suppose that makes sense," murmured Olive, kicking away an acorn that popped up again in the very same spot. "Who're you playing with?"

"Elmer Gorley," said Morton, flopping down onto the grass and glancing over his shoulder at the spot where Elmer supposedly stood. "We're seeing who can jump the farthest. I always win."

"That doesn't sound like much fun. If you know you'll always win, I mean."

Morton squinted up at her. He gave a little shrug. "It's better to play with somebody than nobody."

Olive couldn't think of what to say to that. Except *I'm sorry*. So she did.

"I'm sorry, Morton," she said softly, looking down at the dewy ground near Morton's bare feet. Somehow even Morton's toes looked accusing. "I wasn't being a very good friend . . ."

"Friend?" Morton repeated. He folded his skinny arms across his chest. "I didn't think you wanted to be my friend at all anymore."

Morton's words sank into Olive's stomach like a handful of rocks. She thought about all the times she had chosen the spellbook over him, ignoring him because she had more exciting things to do. She swallowed. It was going to be very scary to say what came next. "I want to be your friend, Morton," she whispered. "I'll try to be a better one. I want to help you. Because I . . . I care about you. And I think I finally found out some things about your family. Important things."

Feeling like someone about to cross a very wobbly bridge, Olive pulled the photograph out of her pocket. She held it out to Morton.

"That's your sister, isn't it?" she asked as Morton frowned down at the photograph. "Lucinda? Or Lucy, for short?"

Morton didn't answer.

"And that's Annabelle McMartin with her. The Old Man's granddaughter."

Morton gave a little twitch.

"The one who grew up in my house, and who got out of her portrait"—Olive coughed, deciding not to mention *how* she'd gotten out—"and who tried to trap us, inside that painting of the forest . . ."

Morton still stared silently at the photograph.

"They were friends, weren't they? Annabelle and Lucinda?" Olive asked, her voice almost a whisper. "And Lucinda wanted to—"

Morton hopped to his feet as though he'd been pinched. "Don't you talk about my sister like that!" he shouted.

"Like *what?*" asked Olive, stunned. "I just think I know—"

"No you don't!" yelled Morton, clenching his fists. "Lucy wouldn't have done it! It wasn't her! You don't know that! You don't know ANYTHING!!"

"Well, I sure don't know *what you're TALKING ABOUT!*" Olive yelled back.

Along Linden Street, a few curious faces popped through open windows.

"She wouldn't—" Morton shouted, choking on a sob. He whirled toward Olive. "You're not *helping*!" he yelled. "You just come in here because you're bored, you make me feel bad, and then you leave again, and I'm stuck here! You just make everything worse!" Morton ran toward the giant oak that towered over the lawn. "Just go away! GO AWAY!!"

"Fine!" yelled Olive. And, because there wasn't anything else to do, she kicked a pile of acorns as hard as she could, sending them clacking and clattering into the street before they turned and rolled back into their original places. But before Olive could stalk into the street herself, the cats popped up, blocking her way.

"Don't give up on him, miss," said Leopold softly.

"Do you want me to climb up and wrestle him down for you?" offered Harvey, looking toward the oak tree with an eager glint in his eyes.

"No," Olive sighed. She tugged exasperatedly at her hair for a moment, rolled her eyes at the purple sky, took a deep breath, and spun around, heading back toward the oak tree.

Morton had disappeared among the leaves. Olive moved closer to the trunk, looking up into the branches with an expression that was as sweet and patient as she could possibly make it.

"Morton?" she called.

An acorn thwapped her on the crown of her head.

"Ow!" Olive shouted, rubbing her scalp. "Morton, that really hurt!"

For a second, there was no answer. Then a voice high in the branches muttered, "Good."

Holding her hands protectively over her head, Olive scanned the leaves again. "Look," she began, "I'm not asking about this to upset you. I need your help, Morton. Please."

The tree gave an angry *hmmph* sound.

"I'm sure your sister loved you, Morton," said Olive. "In fact, I think . . . I think she *still* loves you. But the McMartins have a way of making people do things they wouldn't normally do." She glanced over her shoulder at the bright green eyes of Leopold and Harvey. "They can make us hurt the people we really love."

The branches began to rustle. As Olive watched,

Morton's feet appeared, followed by the rest of his nightshirt-covered body and, finally, his distrustful face. He stopped a few feet above her head.

"Morton," Olive began, "I didn't mean to make you mad—"

But Morton cut her off before she could finish. "Lucinda used to be nice to me," he said. "She made me things. Like pancakes. She fixed my socks when they got holes. But then she made friends with . . . with . . ." Morton seemed to struggle with the words. ". . . With the people next door. That girl. The mean one. And then she wasn't nice anymore."

Olive watched while Morton dropped from the low branches to the ground. He crouched down, picking up an acorn and throwing it with all his might down the street. "Mama and Papa said she couldn't go over to the stone house anymore. And then Lucy got really mad. And then the bad stuff started—" Morton stopped. He picked up the same acorn again, but this time his throw was weaker. The acorn bobbled along the pavement a few yards away, then popped back up in its assigned place.

Olive held very still.

"I didn't think she'd really hurt them . . ." whispered Morton. He was staring at the ground, so Olive couldn't see his face.

Olive dropped to her knees in front of him. "Morton,

maybe she didn't," she whispered back. "Maybe the McMartins put them in a painting somewhere."

Morton's eyes widened. His eyebrows rose until it looked like they were trying to escape into his hair. "*Where?*"

"Well, that's the problem. We don't know where," said Olive, wishing with all her heart for something better to say. "But if anybody knows, it's your sister. And she's still alive. Sort of. She's . . . like you."

Morton's eyebrows pulled together, turning his face into a crinkled moon.

"She lives next door," Olive went on. "She's a painting, but nobody else knows it. Just me and the cats and Rutherford."

"Rutherford?" Morton's frown deepened.

"A neighbor boy who's been helping me," Olive plowed on. "But Mrs. Nivens—I mean, Lucinda—is probably not going to tell *us* where your parents are. She's still trying to help Annabelle McMartin."

"It's true, Agent M," said Harvey, zooming across the lawn. "She's already retrieved the evidence and is planning to bring down the government *from the inside.*"

"He means that she has the painting with Annabelle in it," Olive translated. "And she's going to let her out."

"If she hasn't done it already," Harvey put in helpfully.

Olive glared at the cat. "Thank you, Agent 1-800."

She turned back to Morton. "That's why we need you. You know your way around that house. You can help us sneak in. You can help us search. And maybe if Lucinda sees you . . ." Olive finished slowly, "Who knows?"

Still frowning, Morton got to his feet. He kicked at the ground and folded his scrawny arms across his chest. Then he nodded.

"I can take care of her," he said. "She's just my big sister."

As it turned out, distracting Mr. and Mrs. Dunwoody while the cats smuggled Morton out of the painting was much easier than Olive had feared.

After lunch, the three Dunwoodys went out to the front porch to finish their lemonade and cookies. While her parents rocked on the porch swing, Olive stood next to the railing, tapping her foot impatiently. Near her tapping toes, a chain of ants was climbing up onto the porch, using each other's bodies as bridges to get across the gaps in the floorboards in order to reach a cluster of cookie crumbs.

"How do ants know to do that?" she wondered aloud.

Mr. Dunwoody hopped up from the porch swing. He bent over the chain of ants. "Ah, yes," he breathed, his eyes brightening behind his thick glasses. "Fascinating, isn't it? Even without any central system of control, communication of the various entities enables them to reach a common goal."

Mrs. Dunwoody got up and peered eagerly over her husband's shoulder. "Yes," she agreed. "It requires message passing, but in this case, each autonomous computational entity can only communicate with its nearest neighbors. It does make one wonder what sort of pattern emerges . . ."

Mr. and Mrs. Dunwoody's eyes met.

Olive tiptoed backward toward the door as her parents took each other's hands and began to whisper romantically about cellular automata and parallel computations.

"Is it all right if Rutherford Dewey comes over?" she asked just before slipping inside.

Her parents nodded distractedly.

Olive bolted up the stairs, signaled to the cats, who were waiting in the hallway, Leopold standing at attention with his chin upraised, and Harvey hiding, spy-style, behind the banister, and then rushed back downstairs to the telephone as the two cats leaped through the frame into the painting of Linden Street.

Within ten minutes, Rutherford, Morton, Leopold, and Harvey were assembled in Olive's bedroom. Olive closed the door behind Rutherford and gestured to

Morton, who was sitting on the bed with his knees up and his chin tucked firmly against his chest, looking like a hedgehog in defensive position.

"Morton, this is Rutherford, from down the street. Rutherford, this is my friend Morton . . . from the painting outside my door."

Morton's eyes flashed to Rutherford. He stared at him for a few moments, not speaking. In the bright daylight that filtered through the windows, his painted skin looked slick and streaked, and his old-fashioned nightshirt seemed strangely out of place.

Rutherford, never at a loss for words, broke the silence. "Hello," he said. "I'm Rutherford Dewey. I live two houses away. I'm an expert on the Middle Ages, and a semi-expert on dinosaurs, so I plan to eventually become a history professor, unless I decide to become a vertebrate paleontologist, focusing on aquatic dinosaurs. But if you've been in a painting for eighty-some years, like Olive says, you might not have heard much about dinosaurs. Then again, the word *dinosaur* was coined in 1842, and the so-called Great American Dinosaur Rush happened in the late nineteenth century, so maybe you did. In any case, just call me Rutherford."

Morton was frowning at Rutherford now. Olive couldn't tell if this was because he disliked him, or because he was trying very hard to follow everything Rutherford had said.

"How old are you?" Morton demanded.

"Eleven and a half," said Rutherford.

"Oh," said Morton, looking disappointed. He stiffened up again. "But do you know how to spell *pneumonia*?"

"P-N-E-U-M-O-N-I-A," said Rutherford.

"That's right," Morton mumbled. He glared at Rutherford out of the corner of one eye. "Did you . . ." he began, hesitating before playing his trump card, ". . . did you ever win first prize in a sack race?"

"A sack race?" repeated Rutherford. "No, I can't say that I have."

Morton looked considerably relieved. Still, he kept one eye on Rutherford as everyone settled down to work.

Both the bedspread and the floor were crowded with sketches, hand-drawn maps, and strategy charts, and yet Horatio's absence made the room feel empty. The spellbook—and the note Olive had left with it—had disappeared. Even though Horatio had done as she requested, the fact that he stayed out of sight meant that he still hadn't forgiven her . . . and she was starting to wonder if he ever would.

Leopold gazed down at the papers like a general in his war room and tried to make only gruff, important observations. Harvey, on the other hand, was beside himself with excitement.

"Hey," he panted, scrambling to the center of the rug and knocking a notebook aside. "Hey, everyone. We could call ourselves The Unpettables. Get it? Like The Untouchables?"

No one answered.

"Or how about the CIA, for Cats In Action?"

"I think someone is already using that acronym," said Rutherford.

"That's why it *works*," insisted Harvey. Rutherford looked skeptical. "Okay, fine. No CIA. What about The Mata Hairies?"

"Harvey, we need to focus," said Olive, wishing for the thousandth time that Horatio were there to keep things under control. "We still haven't solved the first problem. How do we make sure that Mrs. Nivens is out of the house and *stays* out of the house while we search it?"

"Perhaps we can cause some kind of distraction," said Rutherford.

"We could lead an advance battalion to the front of the house, and while the enemy is engaged, we approach on foot, capturing the house from the rear!" proposed Leopold.

"What battalion?" said Olive.

"Oh," said Leopold, crestfallen. "Yes. I see."

"Leave it to the special agent," said Harvey, his eyes lighting up. "I'll infiltrate the foreign territory under cover of night, and then—*we'll set her front yard on fire!*"

"No," said Olive.

Harvey pouted.

"We need a simpler kind of distraction—something that won't draw the attention of any of the other neighbors, but that still gives us enough time to search the house," said Rutherford.

Olive and Leopold nodded in agreement.

"And if that doesn't work, I can poison her with an MI6 standard-issue arsenic ink pen!" said Harvey.

"*NO,*" said Olive.

Harvey harrumphed.

Everyone was quiet for a minute, thinking.

"We could always use the grimoire . . ." said Rutherford.

"No," said Olive. "No, we can't." She glanced at Leopold out of the corner of her eye. He had tensed at the word *grimoire,* turning to look at her. "We're not going to use the book anymore."

"I just thought of another problem," said Rutherford. "It's very likely that Mrs. Nivens knows you'll try to get the spectacles back. What's to stop her from just taking them with her wherever she goes?"

It was a good point. Olive deflated, leaning back against her pillows. "I wish Horatio were here," she said softly.

But Horatio wasn't there.

And he stayed *not there* as the five of them put together their plan, covered Morton in a wide-brimmed fedora and an old trench coat of Mr. Dunwoody's to protect his skin from the sunlight, and hurried down through the house. In the kitchen, Olive slipped a flashlight into her pocket, just in case.

Mr. and Mrs. Dunwoody were still on the front porch, busy with pencils and graphing paper.

"We're playing outside!" shouted Olive, not waiting for an answer before herding the whole group out the back door.

The sky had turned overcast, with a thick haze of clouds blocking out the late-afternoon sun. The air felt still and heavy. Everyone hurried down the steps into the backyard—everyone but Morton. Olive glanced over her shoulder.

Morton was still standing on the porch, gazing across the overgrown backyard toward the upper floors of Mrs. Nivens's house. Except for a weak breeze fluttering the bottom edge of his nightshirt, he didn't move at all.

"Morton?" Olive asked softly. "Are you all right?"

"It looks so different," he whispered. "But it also looks the same."

"Yeah," said Olive. She looked at the house a moment, then climbed back up the steps and held out her hand. "Are you ready?"

Morton nodded. The too-long sleeve of the trench coat reached out, and Morton took Olive's hand.

The five of them slunk along the side of the old stone house and hunched close to the lilac hedge, watching Mrs. Nivens's windows.

"All right," Olive whispered. "Harvey, remember to keep both eyes on Rutherford. If anything goes wrong, try to alert us immediately."

Harvey, decked from head to toe in a camouflage of leaves, gave her a sharp nod.

"Rutherford, just keep her busy for as long as you can."

"Don't worry about that," said Rutherford. "I'm very seldom at a loss for things to say."

"Everybody ready?" Olive asked, trying to keep her voice bold and cheery.

The four others nodded. Rutherford set off toward Mrs. Nivens's front door. Harvey slunk along behind him, keeping his belly smooshed against the ground, dodging behind every available plant or twig. Olive, Morton, and Leopold waited until they heard Rutherford give three loud knocks. Then they darted across the backyard, around the far side of the tall gray house, and huddled in a clump of hydrangeas where they had a clear view of Rutherford positioned on the front stoop.

Mrs. Nivens's footsteps made ladylike clicks as she

walked up the hall to the front door. From their position behind the hydrangeas, they couldn't quite see her, but they could hear her voice.

"Well, Rutherford Dewey!" she exclaimed in her sweetest tone. Morton started as though someone had given him an electric shock. "What can I do for you this afternoon?"

"Hello, Mrs. Nivens," said Rutherford, very, very loudly. "I'm trick-or-treating."

"Oh." Mrs. Nivens hesitated. "But Rutherford, dear, Halloween is more than two months away."

"I know," Rutherford answered as Leopold slunk out of the lowest branches and headed toward the house. "You could say that I'm practicing. I'm planning the ideal route in order to visit the greatest number of houses in the least amount of time, with little or no backtracking."

"I see," said Mrs. Nivens, sounding as though she certainly *didn't*. "And why aren't you wearing a costume?"

"As I said, this is merely a practice round. A dress rehearsal. But without the dress. A pre–dress rehearsal, I suppose you could say." Rutherford's loud, fast voice covered up the soft rustle of grass as Olive, Morton, and Leopold crawled toward the house. "So . . . Trick or treat?"

Mrs. Nivens gave an awkward little titter. She was

clearly out of practice at laughing. "Well, you're in luck, Rutherford. I think I may have some Halloween candy left over from last year. I'll be right back."

"Yes," announced Rutherford, speaking even louder than before. "You go and get the candy, *which I assume is in the kitchen,* while I wait right here on the front step."

There was a moment's pause while Mrs. Nivens gave Rutherford a long, confused look. Then there was a creak from the floor and the sound of footsteps clicking down the hall toward the back of the house.

"There's a basement window that latches on the outside," Morton whispered, leading Olive and Leopold along the foundations. "This one. It isn't too far a drop to the floor." Morton tugged the latch and raised the small, rectangular window.

Leopold dove through first. "All clear," he murmured from below.

Olive wriggled through next, feet-first. As her head slid past Morton, who was holding up the window, Morton whispered, "She doesn't really sound like Lucy. But at the same time, she does."

Olive nodded, gave a last wriggle, and plummeted into Mrs. Nivens's basement. Morton was right: The drop wasn't too far, but Olive still managed to land awkwardly, fall onto her hands and knees, and nearly squish Leopold in the process. Morton slipped lightly through behind her. The window clicked shut.

Olive switched on her flashlight and took a look around. A few small windows at the tops of the walls let in the watery gray light from outside. Otherwise, the basement was dark. It was one large, square room, empty except for a gleaming washer and dryer, with a shelf full of detergents set up above.

"This looks different but the same too," whispered Morton.

"Lead the way, sir," said Leopold.

Morton darted through the darkness to a set of creaking wooden steps. Olive and Leopold hurried after him. In spite of his size, Leopold could climb soundlessly. Morton was small and light and seemed to know where to step to keep the stairs from making too much noise, but Olive thundered behind, feeling like a hippo on a ladder made of toothpicks.

"Shh!" hissed Morton as he reached the top of the stairs.

"I'm trying to *shh*!" Olive hissed back.

Morton turned the knob and eased the door open. Olive turned off the flashlight and slipped it back into her pocket. A sliver of light fell over the three of them as they crowded into the gap, peering out. They were looking onto a wood-floored hallway lined with closed doors. In the distance, to their left, an electric light burned.

Rustling sounds came from the kitchen, where Mrs.

Nivens was getting the candy. Then her steps clicked back down the hall, moving fast. Her shadow, with its neatly starched skirt and just as neatly starched hair, flitted toward them. Olive, Leopold, and Morton bolted around the corner into the living room, pressing their backs to the wall.

"Here we are," they heard Mrs. Nivens tell Rutherford cheerily. "Two candy bars. But don't spoil your dinner."

"Actually," said Rutherford, still speaking as though he were addressing someone on the other side of a busy street, "I can't have this kind. I'm allergic to peanuts. The reaction can be quite severe."

"Well, just take the other one, then. It doesn't have peanuts in it."

"The thing is," Rutherford said, "I can't have anything that contains peanut-derived products, or that even came into contact with anything that contains peanuts or peanut-derived products. You should probably check the ingredients on the bag, just to be safe."

Mrs. Nivens let out a breath that Olive could hear all the way around the corner. "All right," she said, her voice losing some of its cheery polish. "I'll just go do that."

"In fact," Rutherford shouted after Mrs. Nivens, "you should probably make sure that the candy came from a factory that doesn't process any peanut products at all. If it doesn't say so on the package, you might want to call the company. Just to be safe."

In the kitchen, Mrs. Nivens muttered something that Olive couldn't quite make out.

Olive, Morton, and Leopold peeped out into the hall. Muffled sounds still came from the kitchen. With a soldierly nod, Leopold signaled that the hallway was clear. Morton edged around the front wall of the living room, turned to the left, and darted lightly up the staircase to the second floor with Leopold at his heels. Meanwhile, Olive slipped across the hall and through the doorway of the room where she'd seen the light burning last night.

The room was empty—empty, that was, except for a long dining table covered with a lacy tablecloth, a set of uncomfortable-looking chairs, and an old-fashioned glass-shaded lamp. Two of the chairs were pulled slightly away from the table, as though they had been recently used. The rest of the room looked as though it hadn't been touched, or even breathed in, for about fifty years. There were no paintings or spectacles to be seen.

Olive edged back into the hall. She could hear Mrs. Nivens thumping cabinet doors in the kitchen. Giving Rutherford a reassuring nod, Olive hurried up the staircase.

She found Morton standing in the upstairs hallway. He stared from side to side, looking at the blank
walls. "There used to be pictures here," he whispered
as Olive tiptoed up behind him. "And right here, there
was a little table. Mama used to put flowers on it."

Olive nodded, trying to hurry him along. "Where
do you think Lucinda would have hidden the painting?"

But Morton didn't seem to be listening. Still staring up at the empty walls, he trailed forward a few
steps and turned to the right, turning the knob of a
closed door. Its hinges creaked softly as he pushed it
open.

Olive froze. She and Leopold exchanged a glance.
Had Mrs. Nivens heard them? Olive strained to listen
to the voices below. Rutherford's voice was still coming
from the distant front door. She thought she caught
the words "Cretaceous period" and "K-T extinction,"
which meant he was probably in the middle of some
very long explanation. With a nod at Leopold, Olive
followed Morton through the open door.

It was Leopold who remembered to bump the
door shut behind them. Olive was too busy watching
Morton. And Morton was too busy looking around.

The room in which they stood was painted a
pale shade of blue. A small wrought iron bed sat in
one corner, while the opposite wall was lined with a

dresser and a bookshelf. An old wooden wagon sat in one corner, holding a baseball bat, a toy drum, and a somewhat deflated-looking striped ball. Black-and-white pictures were tacked to the walls, many of them cut from newspapers and catalogs—pictures of baseball players and exotic animals and funny old-fashioned cars that looked, to Olive, more like sleds on wheels. The paper of the pictures was yellowed and curling. The bed was perfectly made, all the furniture was dusted, but from the loneliness that hung in the air, Olive could tell that no one had used this room for a very, very long time.

Leopold cleared his throat and nodded toward the door. It was time to move on. Olive glanced around, taking in every corner. There was no painting here.

"Morton—" she began.

Morton didn't turn around. "This is my room," he said softly. "It's just the same. She kept everything just the same."

Olive wrapped her hand around Morton's baggy sleeve. "We have to keep looking, Morton. I don't know how much longer Rutherford can keep her busy."

Morton gave an absent nod. "You go," he whispered, staring at the little iron bed. A small blue horse made out of corduroy was lying on the pillows. "I'll be there in a minute."

With a worried sigh, Olive turned to the door. "Stay

with him," she whispered to Leopold before sidling back out into the upstairs hall.

Olive edged along the wall, starfish-style. She could hear Rutherford's voice still rambling in the distance. When her fingers hit the cold brass of the next doorknob, Olive opened the door, backed smoothly through it, and shut it again behind her.

For a moment, she practically glowed with pride. She had never done anything so gracefully and quietly in her whole life. Even Horatio would have been impressed. Blood was pounding through her body, but Olive's mind felt surprisingly calm and clear. She could do this. Still smiling to herself, she took a look around.

She had backed into a bathroom. Like the living room and hallway, it was spotless and shiny. The tiles around the bathtub gleamed, the faucets didn't drip, the mirror didn't have a single fleck of toothpaste on it. Even the dish full of seashell-shaped soaps was so clean it looked new, as though it had never been touched at all.

There were no spectacles to be seen. Olive checked the drawers and the medicine cabinet, just to make sure. But they were all completely empty. This seemed odd at first, until Olive realized that Mrs. Nivens, being a painting, wouldn't need to use a bathroom or anything in it. All of this was only for her nonexistent guests, like most of the bedrooms in the Dunwoodys' house. The difference was that Mrs. Nivens obviously *cleaned* for her nonexistent guests.

Olive peeked back out into the hall.

"*Coelacanth* actually means 'hollow spine,' in Greek. But the spine of the coelacanth isn't really hollow, it's a sort of cartilage tube full of fluid." These were the words Olive could hear Rutherford saying, although to Mrs. Nivens, they probably sounded something like this: "Butthespynovthesealacanthisntreallyhollowitzasordovcardilidgetoobfullovfluid." Rutherford's voice buzzed on as Olive slipped toward the third door. "Another interesting thing about the coelacanth is that it gives birth to live young. Well, technically, they're ovoviviparous . . ."

She had just placed her hand on the knob when, behind her, someone let out a gasp.

Morton stood in the hall, the blue horse clutched in his arms. He shook his head emphatically and then broke into a run, hurrying toward her. Leopold bounded silently along beside him.

"You can't go in there!" Morton whispered once he'd reached the doorway. "That's Lucy's room!"

"We have to check everywhere," Olive argued under her breath. "Besides, where would she be more likely to hide things than her own bedroom?"

"No! She'll be really mad!" Morton argued back, trying to pry Olive's hands off the doorknob.

Maybe it was the painted slipperiness of Morton's hands, or maybe Olive was stronger, but somehow Morton lost his grip and staggered backward into the hall. Suddenly fighting a one-sided battle, Olive staggered backward too, pulling the door open with a much-too-abrupt yank. The heavy door made a low rattling noise against the frame.

Olive held her breath. Morton gave her a horrified look over the head of the blue horse. Leopold froze, doing his best small stuffed panther impression.

Rutherford's clear, rapid voice was still ringing up the stairs. ". . . Of course, by that time ichthyosaurs were extinct, making mosasaurs the dominant ocean predator. Most people aren't aware of this, but ichthyosaurs bore live young, like the coelacanth, except the ichthyosaur also breathed air . . ."

Perhaps Mrs. Nivens hadn't even heard them over the sound of Rutherford's rambling. No footsteps hurried up the stairs; no one shouted, "Who's there?" They were safe.

With Olive leading the way, Leopold marching after her, and Morton trailing reluctantly behind, they edged into Lucinda's bedroom.

It was the neatest room Olive had ever seen. A white lace bedspread covered the bed, looking as clean and fresh as one giant snowflake. Matching white lace curtains hung over the windows, all of their frilly edges evenly spaced. Olive wondered if Mrs. Nivens straightened them with a ruler. The walls were bare, apart from two framed arrangements of dried flowers that looked as though they had been petrified by shock. A row of books with matching pale pink covers lined the bookshelves, surrounded by a collection of delicate porcelain ballerinas and blown glass roses and other things that would have to be dusted with a Q-tip.

And yet, in spite of its neatness, there was something horrible about this room. It was girlish and cold and still, like a rosebud embedded in ice: If it thawed, it would instantly decay. Olive tiptoed across the floor and touched the lacy bedspread with one fingertip. No wonder the room was so neat, she thought. It was a museum. No one slept here, ate stashes of hidden cookies here, had bad dreams here, and woke up to read books by the light of the bedside lamp. No one lived here at all. This room—this whole neat, perfect house—was one gigantic coffin.

Ready to bolt back out into the hall, Olive turned back toward Morton and Leopold. But Morton wasn't looking at her. His eyes were fixed on a full-length, white-framed mirror that stood against the left-hand wall.

"This wasn't here before," he whispered.

Olive hurried to one side of the mirror and Morton

darted to the other. Very carefully, trying to keep its legs from scraping against the polished hardwood floor, they slid the mirror to one side. Behind it, leaning against the spotless white wall, was a painting—a painting in a heavy gold frame.

Olive knew this painting well. It had once hung in her upstairs hall. She had noticed it on her very first visit to the old stone house, and she had known, even then, that there was something strange about it. It was the first painting she had ever explored with the magic spectacles. It was where she had met Morton, and been rescued by the cats, and been chased by a . . . a *thing* made from the ashes of Aldous McMartin. It was a painting of a dark, eerie forest, where a moonlit path disappeared into the bony lace of bare trees. The last time Olive had seen this painting, she had been burying it in her backyard, and the trapped image of Annabelle McMartin had scowled furiously up at her from the canvas. There were still traces of dirt clinging to the painting, stuck in the whorls of the frame.

But where Annabelle's angry face should have been, there was nothing—nothing but the moonlight falling on leaf-strewn stones. Leopold and Morton hurried closer, peering over her shoulders as Olive knelt down in front of the painting.

"Oh, no," Olive breathed.

Nonsensically, she grabbed the sides of the heavy frame and shook it, as though Annabelle might fall back into view like an ant that's been hiding at the edge of an ant farm. Nothing happened. There was no trace of Annabelle anywhere. And if she wasn't in there, it meant that Annabelle McMartin was somewhere . . . out *here*.

"Olive Dunwoody," said a woman's voice.

OLIVE WHIRLED AROUND. Of course, it's very hard to whirl when you're on all fours, so she sort of flopped from her knees into crab-walking position, with her back pressed against the painting. Morton turned as well, tripped on the trailing hem of the trench coat, and fell into Olive's lap. Leopold hopped in front of the two of them and bared his teeth, hissing.

Annabelle McMartin glided gracefully through the doorway.

The last time Olive had seen Annabelle, her pretty face had been twisted with rage and her long brown hair had blown wildly in a cold wind. The Annabelle now standing in front of her looked like a different person. She looked like the young woman from the portrait again; the woman who had sweetly invited

Olive to tea and listened to all her secrets; the woman who had paddled Olive into the middle of a raging lake and left her there to drown.

Each painted strand of Annabelle's hair had been smoothed and fastened in place. Her string of pearls had been straightened, and her frilly antique dress was gone, replaced by a prim skirt and blouse set of Mrs. Nivens's. But her eyes were the same pools of honey-colored paint, and her mouth, when she smiled, had the same deceptive sweetness.

Olive felt her body freeze. She could almost hear tiny ice cubes clinking in her veins. Morton and Leopold didn't move either.

"You brought your friends," Annabelle went on, turning her tiny smile to Morton and Leopold in turn. "How nice of you, to get them mixed up in all of this again. Hello, Leopold." The cat stiffened. "Hello, Morton. I wondered when I would see you again."

Keeping her arm carefully hidden behind Morton, Olive groped for the flashlight that was wedged in her pocket. But before she could even wrap her shaking hand around it, the flashlight flew out from between her fingers, rolling past Annabelle's feet in their little high heels and out into the hallway.

"That isn't going to work this time," said Annabelle sweetly, lowering her hand. "I'm better prepared for your tricks. And, obviously, you haven't come up with anything new." She laughed, a light, gentle laugh. "In fact, you've done almost *exactly* what we wanted you to do. You used the book, estranged your friends, dug up the painting, *brought* us the spectacles. If you had jumped off of the roof last night, it would have been a bit easier, but . . . Oh, well." Annabelle sighed lightly, as though a batch of cookies she'd been baking had gotten a little too brown. "We can handle it this way too, I suppose." She took a step closer, her eyes traveling from Olive to Morton and Leopold. "Three birds with one stone, as they say."

"It's *two* birds," blurted Morton.

Annabelle's smile widened. "Well, aren't you irritating," she told Morton, her inflection the same as if she'd said *Well, aren't you precious.* "I can see why your sister wanted to get rid of you."

Morton hopped out of Olive's lap. He squared his shoulders, squeezing the blue horse tightly in his arms. "She did not," he said loudly. "You made her do bad things. Lucy loved us. You *made* her do it." He stomped his foot, and the fedora on his round head tipped rakishly over one ear.

"Let's ask her about that, shall we?" Annabelle, still smiling, made a little sign in the air with one hand. There was the sound of a door slamming, followed by footsteps clicking quickly up the stairs.

"Yes, Annabelle?" panted Mrs. Nivens, hurrying through the bedroom doorway. She halted suddenly, as if she'd hit an invisible wall. Her eyes flicked from Olive, still leaning against the painting, to the large black cat positioned protectively before her, to the small, tufty-haired, trench-coated boy clutching a blue corduroy horse.

"Morton," she gasped. Her hands flew up to her chest, clutching handfuls of her neatly ironed blouse. Olive would have worried about Mrs. Nivens's heart, but she reminded herself that Mrs. Nivens didn't have one— not anymore.

"Lucy?" Morton whispered. He stepped closer to her, staring up. A small frown creased his broad white forehead. "You look so . . . *different.*"

Mrs. Nivens's glassy eyes were wide. A smile trembled on her lips, jerking them sideways as she spoke. "And you look exactly the same, Morton."

Watching her, Olive wondered if Mrs. Nivens was about to cry. But of course she *couldn't* cry. Not real tears, anyway. Only one thing seemed certain: For the moment, Mrs. Nivens had forgotten about everyone else in the room. As subtly as she could, Olive nudged Leopold with her foot and then nodded toward the hall, where the flashlight lay. Leopold edged slowly toward Morton's side. Olive tried to shift onto her knees, getting ready to run, if necessary, but Annabelle's eyes honed in on her, their painted pools wary and bright. Olive froze.

"Was it you?" Morton was asking, his voice still not much more than a whisper. "Was it? Did you really ask the Old Man to take me away?"

"I told him not to hurt you," said Mrs. Nivens, sidestepping the question. "And he didn't. See?" Mrs. Nivens crouched in front of Morton, bringing their faces level. For a second, Olive could almost picture the Lucinda Nivens of eighty years ago, kneeling down to speak eye to eye with her little brother. "You get to live forever. Just like me."

Morton shook his head. He shook it harder and harder, until his face became a blur. "No," he said, stopping. "I'm just *stuck*. I'm stuck being *nine* forever." He glared up at his sister. "But at least I'm not stuck being an ugly old lady."

"Morton!" gasped Mrs. Nivens.

"What? Are you going to *tell* on me?" taunted Morton. "It was always *Morton, the bad boy* and *Lucinda, the good girl*. But you were just pretending. You were tricking them." Morton choked, the anger in his voice suddenly trickling away. "What did he do with them?" he asked softly. "Where are Mama and Papa?"

Mrs. Nivens shook her head. "Morton . . ." she began, ". . . I don't know."

"Yes you do," argued Morton. "What did he do to them?"

"He—he put them someplace safe. Like you. He didn't hurt them. I *asked* him not to hurt them—"

"You're so STUPID!" yelled Morton, his body quaking with fury. "Why should *he* do what *you* said? Where are they? WHAT HAPPENED TO THEM?"

"Morton, I honestly don't know. Honestly," said Mrs. Nivens, a pleading note slipping into her voice. "Annabelle," she ventured, "do *you* know?"

Annabelle gave a sigh. Leopold took advantage of her momentarily closed eyes to slip closer to the doorway. "Really, Lucinda," Annabelle said, "you would have to be much less sentimental to even *hope* to become one of us."

"I'm sorry, Annabelle," said Mrs. Nivens, getting swiftly to her feet and backing away from Morton.

There was a sudden loud yowl as Leopold flew through the air, kicked backward by Annabelle's high heel. He landed next to Olive, in front of the painting.

"You know I don't like to fight a lady—" the cat huffed, getting back to his feet and baring his claws.

"Fight me?" Annabelle interrupted him with a laugh. "Once we've taken care of these two, I will deal with you, Leopold. Now stand aside." Annabelle muttered something and made a sweeping motion with her arm.

Dragged by an invisible leash, Leopold slid backward across the floor and smacked into the opposite wall. There he stuck, hissing and growling, as though his fur had been Velcro-ed to the plaster.

"Now, take out the spectacles, Lucinda."

Obediently, Mrs. Nivens pulled the spectacles out of her skirt pocket. Faint daylight leaking through the lace curtains glinted softly on their lenses. Olive's heart gave a desperate leap before flopping back into its place again. Even if she could get the spectacles away from Mrs. Nivens, there was no way she could physically overpower both women. She chewed the inside of her cheek so hard she could taste blood.

"What are you going to do?" Mrs. Nivens asked in a very small voice, glancing at Annabelle.

"Only what they did to me," said Annabelle. "We're going to put the two of them in this painting. Then we're going to destroy it before they manage to get out and annoy us further."

"Destroy it?" Mrs. Nivens repeated.

"Yes," Annabelle said lightly. "We're going to burn it."

Morton let out a squeak and backed quickly toward Olive. She pulled him down beside her, wrapping her arm around his shoulders and pressing her back against the painting to stay as far from Annabelle as possible. She shot a look at Leopold, who was writhing and hissing wildly against the wall.

"You can't do that," said Olive, trying to sound angry rather than terrified, and not quite succeeding.

Annabelle's prettily arched eyebrows went up. "Olive, dear," she said sweetly, "you got yourself into this." She turned to Lucinda. "Put on the spectacles."

Mrs. Nivens hesitated. "Why does *he* have to go in?" she whispered, tilting her head toward Morton, who was huddled tight against Olive's shoulder. "Couldn't we just put him back in some other painting?"

"No, we couldn't," said Annabelle. "So much senti-ment, Lucinda. Do you want to be part of our family, or not? Do you want me to teach you, or not?" Her voice was losing its sweetness. "Are you loyal to us . . . or not?"

Mrs. Nivens wavered, glancing at Morton. "But what has he done? It's all Olive's fault. Why does Morton have to be punished too?"

"Because *I said so*," said Annabelle, very low, stepping closer to Mrs. Nivens. They were almost exactly the same height, but something about Annabelle's voice or her way of moving made her seem twice as large as Mrs. Nivens. "Give me the spectacles, if you're too weak to do this." In the next second, she had tugged them out of Mrs. Nivens's unresisting hand.

Annabelle crossed the room so quickly that Olive couldn't even squirm out of the way. Before she knew it, Annabelle was crouching in front of her, with her brown eyes glowing behind the spectacles' lenses, and her cold, painted hand pressed against Olive's chest.

The moment Annabelle touched her, Olive felt the canvas behind her back turn to jelly. Her spine began to sink inward. The cool night breeze of the painted forest slipped through the fabric of her shirt. Beside her, Morton was being shoved backward too, fighting to pull himself upright again.

"Morton!" Olive yelled. "Grab on to the frame!"

Morton's fingers, lost inside the trench coat sleeves, scrabbled at the heavy gold frame. Olive braced him with one arm and reached out for the frame's other side, clamping her hand around it. Across the room, Leopold hissed and struggled helplessly.

"Help!" Morton shouted. "Lucy, help!"

But Mrs. Nivens didn't move. She stood still, several steps behind Annabelle, looking more than ever like something carved out of butter and unable to move on its own.

"Shh," whispered Annabelle, her lips curved in a sweet little smile. "Let's not disturb the neighbors."

Her cold, strong hands wrapped around Olive's and Morton's throats. Both of them let go of the frame, trying to pry her fingers away, and immediately began to tilt backward into the dark and windy forest.

"NO!" Olive choked, thrashing and kicking in an attempt to knock the spectacles off of Annabelle's

smiling face. The muscles in her stomach and her legs were burning with effort, and it was getting harder and harder to breathe. "Harvey! Rutherford! Help!" But Annabelle's reach was long, and she kept her icy hand clamped tight around Olive's throat, forcing her into the painting.

"Help!" Olive screamed again, just before the upper half of her body toppled backward. Annabelle gave her a powerful shove, and Olive found herself suddenly hanging upside down inside the painting, with her legs locked around the bottom of the frame as though it were a rung on the monkey bars. Cold air and darkness washed over her. The bony trees hung, upside down, in front of her, beckoning with their bare branches. Just above her, she glimpsed Morton's terrified face and thrashing arms as Annabelle tried to push him in after her.

"No," she heard someone say. "You can't do this to him!"

Annabelle's face vanished from the frame. Morton reached out, grabbing Olive's arm, and she managed to swing herself up into sitting position. Holding on to each other, they scrambled over the edge of the frame. Olive felt the forest wind die away as the canvas turned solid behind them.

Mrs. Nivens had grasped Annabelle by the back of the blouse, yanking her toward the center of the bedroom. As Olive and Morton watched, huddling against the side of the frame, Annabelle wheeled around and slapped Mrs. Nivens, hard, on the cheek. Then, holding her by both wrists, Annabelle shoved Mrs. Nivens backward across the floor, toward the painting.

"Climb in," Annabelle said. "You and your little brother can burn together. It will be nice and cozy."

"Wait," said Mrs. Nivens, her voice rising, shrill and breathy. "You said—you promised to teach me, to take me into your family. I've served you all this time; I brought you back—"

Annabelle laughed a light, tinkling laugh, like bits of broken crystal falling to a stone floor. "*You*, Lucinda?" She shook her head. "If tonight has shown us anything, it's that *you* are not the sort of apprentice we need." Annabelle flicked her wrist, mumbling a few words that Olive couldn't catch. Floating above the tips of her fingers appeared a small, shimmering ball of fire. "Now, climb in, or I'll burn your little brother right here."

Morton gave a strangled yelp. A flood of furious words crashed through Olive's brain, but she couldn't think of anything to say that wouldn't just make Annabelle angrier. She wrapped her arms protectively around Morton and felt the little canvas bag tucked inside her shirt shift against her skin.

"I—p-please, Annabelle," Mrs. Nivens stammered

as Annabelle steered her toward the painting. "Don't do this. We've been friends since we were children. I—"

Annabelle gave a light, irritated sigh. "That's enough, Lucinda. *Get in*."

But Mrs. Nivens didn't—or maybe couldn't—move.

The little shimmering ball of fire floated a few inches higher above Annabelle's hand. "It's your choice," she said. Then, before Olive could move or think or even be sure what was happening, Annabelle flicked her wrist, and the ball of flames shot across the room, straight at Morton.

25

OLIVE HAD ALWAYS assumed that if Mrs. Nivens moved too quickly—that was, if she was even *capable* of moving quickly—she would break into pieces, like a frozen stick of butter. But as it turned out, Mrs. Nivens *could* move quickly. Very quickly.

Morton and Olive hadn't even had time to duck out of the way before Mrs. Nivens had thrown herself in front of them. The ball of flames struck her in the chest, bursting like a firework into shafts of sparkling color. Flames rippled across her arms, up into her neatly combed hair, down to the tips of her high-heeled shoes. Aldous McMartin had let out a terrifying shriek when the light from Olive's camping lantern destroyed him, but Lucinda Nivens just gave an indignant gasp, as if someone *very rude* had tossed a candy wrapper into her rosebushes. Then, in one sudden bluish puff, Mrs. Nivens was nothing more than a scorch mark on the otherwise spotless bedroom floor.

Morton screamed. Olive dodged in front of him, trying to keep him both from running at Annabelle and from getting a closer look at the scorch mark.

"Oil paint," explained Annabelle with a little shrug. "It burns so quickly." She raised her hand again, and another shimmering ball of blue and yellow flames formed above her fingertips. "Flesh doesn't burn quite so fast." She smiled. "But you'll see that for yourself, Olive."

Annabelle moved closer, the ball of flames flickering, its light reflected in both lenses of the spectacles. "Let's do this neatly, inside the painting, shall we?" she said, turning her falsely sweet smile from Olive to Morton, barricaded behind her. "It's what Lucinda would have wanted."

That seemed to be enough for Morton.

"You're a BAD LADY!" he screamed, diving out from behind Olive before she could stop him. He grabbed Annabelle by the arm, shaking her furiously.

"Hang on, Morton!" Olive screamed.

One of Annabelle's arms was still locked in Morton's grip, and although she tried to defend herself with the other, Olive had gotten a head start. She leaped at Annabelle, arms out, clawing at Annabelle's painted face. Olive felt the cold slipperiness of Annabelle's skin, and then the familiar glass and metal of the spectacles was closed safely in her fist.

With a growl, Annabelle knocked both Morton and Olive backward, so that they landed in a pile, with Olive on top, holding the spectacles in both hands. The blue corduroy horse slid out of Morton's grasp and glided away across the polished floorboards.

"The spectacles don't matter, you stupid little girl," Annabelle snarled. "I can get rid of you just as easily out here. Watch." Annabelle flicked back her wrist, and the ball of flames zoomed toward Olive's chest. Beneath her, Morton gave a scream. Olive squinched her eyes shut and braced for the fire to strike her.

It hit her like the blast of air from a hair dryer, rippling against her shirt quite pleasantly before dispersing and fading away. The little canvas bag around her neck hung, warm and safe, against her upper ribs. Olive opened her eyes. The fire was gone.

Annabelle's eyes widened. Her smile disappeared. "What?" she whispered.

Olive clambered to her feet, pulling Morton up after her and blockading him with her body. She pushed the spectacles into his hand. "Stay right behind me," she said over her shoulder. Morton stared back at her, his face a rumpled mixture of anger, surprise, and confusion. "I'll protect you," she promised.

"Olive!" shouted a voice from the doorway—a voice with a faint British accent.

Olive turned.

Standing at the room's edge were two cats: one with splotchy fur covered by black paint and dead leaves . . . and one with a rich orange coat that glinted in a temporary shaft of light from the setting sun.

"Horatio!" she whispered. She could feel her heart swelling, lifting until she thought her whole body might rise right off of the ground.

And, in that split second while Olive's guard was down, Annabelle hurled a flickering ball of fire at Morton.

It struck him with a soft hiss. Flames rippled up the lapels and down the sleeves of Mr. Dunwoody's old trench coat, spreading like unraveling threads. Like his sister, Morton didn't scream. He only let out a soft gasp, standing frozen inside a shell of flames.

Time seemed to stretch until it was barely moving forward at all. Olive watched the fire glide over the fabric of the trench coat. She watched Harvey and Horatio spring forward. She watched Horatio's mouth move, but it wasn't until later, when she played the moment back in her mind, that she realized it was forming words: *oil paint*. She watched Morton's wide, trusting eyes turn toward her. And she watched her own hands grasp the burning trench coat, her skin skimming fearlessly through the flames, whipping it away from Morton's body.

Morton spun halfway around and crumpled to the floor. Harvey and Horatio sprang in front of him, hissing, baring their needle-like teeth.

Slowly, time contracted back to its normal size, but still Olive stood, holding the burning trench coat, feeling the fire coast harmlessly over her. There were no thoughts left in her mind at all—only the trusting look in Morton's eyes as she pushed her own arms into the sleeves and pulled the burning coat tight around herself.

She turned toward Annabelle.

Annabelle began to back away toward the window. "Who do you think you are, Olive Dunwoody?" she asked, but her voice wasn't quite as powerful as it had sounded before. "Whose tricks are you stealing now?"

Olive didn't answer. She just stepped closer to Annabelle. Out of the corners of her eyes, she could see streaks of red and gold and blue flames spreading and thickening across her body, but all she felt was a shifting warmth, like when you sit close to a bonfire. The coat's collar was burning near her jaw. Petals of fire licked the edges of her face and danced along her wrists. Flames coasted over the floorboards as Olive walked, dragging the hem of the long coat behind her.

Annabelle shook her head, smirking, but continuing

to back away as Olive came closer. Soon Olive could see the gold flecks of paint in her eyes, the streaked tendrils that made up the waves of her smooth dark hair. The sheen of fire reflected on Annabelle's painted skin.

There was fear in Annabelle's eyes now. "Think carefully, Olive," she said softly. Her back was pressed against the windowsill. "Are you sure this is the side you want to be on?"

"I'm sure," said Olive. She could hear the flames crackling beside her ears. The little canvas bag thumped against her ribs, just above her heart.

Annabelle's eyes narrowed into slits. "You think you're smart enough to outdo our whole family, our centuries of power, all on your own?"

Olive could feel four other sets of eyes watching her: Leopold's, Harvey's, and Horatio's bright green eyes, and Morton's, pale and blue, following her every move. "I'm not on my own," she said.

She raised both arms, like someone waiting for a hug. Her burning sleeves were inches away from Annabelle's painted skin. "Tell me where Morton's parents are," she said.

Annabelle shook her head. A wisp of her sweet smile returned. "Olive Dunwoody," she sighed, "you're just not smart enough for this."

Olive stepped closer.

There was a shattering, crashing sound as Annabelle swung her fist, smashing the window behind her. The lacy curtains flapped and wavered. The curtain rod clattered to the floor. A rush of evening air filled the room, blowing out the flames that rippled up and down the trench coat. Something strange happened in that instant, as Lucinda Nivens's perfect bedroom filled with fresh summer air and falling curtains and bits of broken glass. It felt to Olive as though a spell had been broken, or a sheet of ice had melted, and everything was suddenly alive, awake, and changing. And then, before the first fragments of glass had hit the ground below, Annabelle leaped through the window.

Olive whirled toward Morton. Although its flames had burned out, the coat was still smoldering around her. She tiptoed as near to him as she dared. Morton had retrieved the blue corduroy horse and was curled up around it in a tight, white ball. As far as Olive could see, his nightshirt was intact, and his pale skin appeared whole and unscarred. "Morton, are you all right?" she asked softly.

Morton gave a little nod. He didn't look up. "It hurt for a minute," he whispered. "But then the hurt went away."

Horatio, Harvey, and Leopold, freed from Annabelle's magic, were leaning out through the broken pane. Olive rushed across the room to join them.

Leopold turned toward her, his eyes wide. "Miss, how did you manage—"

Olive pulled the little canvas bag out of the collar of her shirt. "Mrs. Dewey," she whispered. A joyful ripple ran through her as she remembered Mrs. Dewey's words: *Not all magic is dark, you know.* Olive *hadn't* known. But now she wanted to know more. Laying the bag against her shirt, she wedged herself between the cats, looking out the window.

The lawn below was dark. Evening breezes played with the hydrangeas, making the clumps of blossoms nod like heavy heads. A last trace of sunset colored the air with purple smoke. Annabelle had vanished.

"Mission aborted," said Harvey, speaking into an imaginary transistor-watch on his right front paw. "The target has evaded capture and elimination."

"Is she gone?" asked Olive, craning over the shards of broken glass.

"No," said Horatio quietly. "She's waiting. Hiding somewhere. Not gone for good."

"Oh," said Olive. Through the wisps of smoke that rose from her body, she looked out over Linden Street, at the lights glowing softly from houses where people were making dinner and curling up on couches and *not* immolating each other. "I didn't think so."

"This isn't your fault, Olive," said Horatio. And then, before Olive could feel *too* comforted, he added, "That is, not all of it. We"—Horatio paused, looking extremely uncomfortable—"we distracted you by arriving at a most inconvenient moment."

Olive looked down at Horatio. He didn't meet her eyes, but having the three cats there, surrounding her, made everything feel okay again. Almost. "I'm glad you came," she told him. "How did you know where to find us, anyway?"

"Harvey came to—"

"Agent 1-800," Harvey corrected, out of the corner of his mouth.

Horatio rolled his eyes. "Yes, *Agent 1-800* came to get me. Between his ravings about 'bread in a breadbox' and 'wax in an ear,' I was able to glean a few actual facts about what was going on."

"Horatio . . ." Olive swallowed, gazing toward the comforting lights glowing in houses across the street. "I'm sorry that I let the book come between us. I'm sorry that I wasn't strong enough, or smart enough . . ."

Horatio shook his head. "The house was looking for ways to manipulate you. It still is." He glanced at Olive, his bright green eyes taking in the little canvas bag that hung against her shirt. "Whatever mistakes you've made, I think you've begun to figure out whom you can trust. It's just taken you a bit longer than it should have."

Olive kicked a shard of sparkling glass. "Did you know about Mrs. Nivens? About her being a painting, I mean?"

"I had my suspicions," Horatio answered, turning to look out at the street. "But I did not know that she was still trying to serve the McMartins. I had thought that Ms. McMartin's death—her refusal to leave any of the house's contents to Lucinda—would have put an end to that misguided madness. For the first time, you appear to have known more than I did, Olive."

At first, this made Olive smile. But then something in Horatio's words made her feel lonely and a little bit afraid—as though she were venturing out by herself into the darkness. And she wasn't sure she wanted to go out there alone.

Taking a deep breath, Olive turned back toward the bedroom.

Morton had uncurled from his defensive ball. He was kneeling on the polished wooden floor, next to the scorch mark. The fedora sat on the floor beside him. His face was tilted downward so that Olive couldn't see his expression, only the top of his head with its nearly white hair. Its wispy tufts shifted in the breeze.

Following Olive, the cats dropped lightly from the windowsill, gathering around Morton and the scorched spot on the floor. Leopold gave it a salute.

"She killed her," Morton said so softly that at first Olive wasn't sure whether she'd heard the words or imagined them. "She's a murderer." He turned to look up at Olive, his eyes wide. "We have to tell the police."

"Morton . . ." Olive began, ". . . I don't think the police would believe us. And, besides, Annabelle didn't really *kill* her. She was just a painting."

"But *I'm* just a—" Morton stopped. He looked back down at the scorch mark.

"Lucinda was still helping the McMartins," Olive rushed on, trying to argue away the strangely guilty feeling that was creeping up into her chest. "She would have let Annabelle trap us and hurt us."

Morton's head moved just the teeniest bit, and Olive knew that he was listening.

"And you wouldn't want to let the McMartins hurt

anybody else the way they hurt you and your parents. Right?"

Morton's head moved in a tiny nod.

Looking down at his stooped, skinny shoulders made Olive want to throw her arms around him and hug him until they both felt better. But maybe Morton wouldn't want her to hug him. Even if Olive sometimes felt like Morton's big sister, she *wasn't* . . . not really. Morton's actual big sister was the scorch mark in front of him on the hardwood floor.

Hesitantly, Olive leaned down and placed her hand on his head. "I'm sorry, Morton."

Morton let out a long breath. "Yeah," he whispered. "I know."

Then, wobbling a little, Morton stood up. His round face glowed in the fading purplish light from the broken window. Never quite meeting Olive's eyes, he wrapped the corduroy horse in his arms.

Olive straightened up. "Let's go home."

As Olive, with the painting under her arm, Morton, disguised in the scorched-but-extinguished coat, and the three cats tiptoed quietly through Mrs. Nivens's back door, Rutherford popped out from behind the clump of birch trees and erupted like a volcano of words.

"She interrupted me!" he exclaimed. "I was right in the middle of explaining the possible evolutionary links of the coelacanth when she told me she had something in the oven and just closed the door in my face. I'm sorry I couldn't detain her any longer. I've been trying to get insi—"

"It's all right," Olive interrupted. "She's gone now. For good." Morton shifted uncomfortably behind her.

"I see," said Rutherford. "And Annabelle McMartin?"

"She's gone too. But not for good."

Rutherford nodded. "Well," he said after a pause, "we can consider a logical plan of action later. For now, I should be getting home, or my grandmother will worry."

"Bye," said Olive. She touched the little canvas bag that still hung around her neck. "Thank you for this. For everything. And tell Mrs. Dewey thank you too."

Rutherford nodded at the bag. "The charm wears off, remember. You might as well eat the macaroon before it gets stale. And you can keep the knight."

"Okay," said Olive slowly, wondering again how many things Rutherford might know about magic that he wasn't telling her. "Will I—will I see you again sometime?"

"Naturally," said Rutherford, looking surprised. "I'm just two doors away; it would be very unlikely that you *wouldn't* see me. And you know how to summon me if you need me." With a gallant bow, he turned away and disappeared with a twitch of the birch trees. Olive glanced around the darkening backyard. The neat rows of plants and the perfectly trimmed grass were fading into the blue-black air. With no one to neaten and trim them, it wouldn't be long before they vanished entirely. Mrs. Nivens's house seemed to lean toward her, ghostly and accusing, dark and empty. It would remain dark and empty now, just like its mirror version inside the painting of Linden Street.

"Carry on, miss," said Leopold softly from somewhere near her knees.

Olive nodded and led the way back through the lilac hedge into her own backyard.

"Is that you, Olive?" her mother called from the kitchen as Olive, Morton, and the three cats slipped through the back door.

"It's me," Olive called back. Morton and the cats darted silently up the stairs.

"Good. You were almost late for dinner," said Mrs. Dunwoody, smiling at Olive from the kitchen doorway, her hands filled with a stack of plates. "You have just"—she glanced over her shoulder at the microwave clock—"one minute before everything is on the table. Go wash your hands."

"I'll be right down," Olive called over her shoulder, hurrying after her friends to the second floor.

The nail where the painting of the forest had hung was still stuck firmly in its spot. Olive hoisted the heavy frame and hooked it over the edge of the nail. She stepped back, looking at the canvas. The forest lay under its unchanging moon, the white path disappeared between the trees, and the painting was back where it belonged. In spite of the bad memories the picture brought with it, Olive felt better knowing that it was safe inside the big stone house, where no one else could learn its secrets.

She reached out to give the painting a last straightening nudge. The frame didn't move. She paused, then wrapped her fingers around its edge, pulling one way and then the other. Nothing. Heart pounding, Olive hurried to her right, toward the painting of Linden Street, and pushed and pulled on its frame as hard as she could. It didn't move either. She had known it wouldn't. And she knew it would be the same with every other painting in the house, just as it had been when the Dunwoodys first moved in. Olive's hands slipped weakly off the edge of the frame. With Annabelle on the loose, Elsewhere must have regained some of its power.

Olive slumped against the wall, too exhausted to be surprised. The fury that had coursed through her body while she faced Annabelle was trickling away, and now Olive felt floppy and fuzzy and ready to just curl up in a ball someplace dark. She was tired of being afraid. She was tired of fighting. She was tired of *everything*. Raising her heavy head, she glanced back up at the painting of Linden Street.

In the distance, through a veil of mist, she thought she could see the people trapped inside. They rocked on their porches in the never-ending twilight; they gazed out of windows at a view that never changed. She could see the empty gray hulk of Morton's house, far away—the house Morton would have to go back to, all alone.

But he *wasn't* all alone.

The thought flared up inside of Olive like a tiny white fire. Morton still had her. And she had him. And they had the cats—even though Olive had almost lost them. And Rutherford. And Mrs. Dewey. Olive even had two parents who were waiting downstairs at that very minute to heap her plate with perfectly symmetrical portions of meatloaf and mashed potatoes. And maybe . . . somehow, somewhere . . . Morton had two parents who were waiting for him too.

Olive wrapped her fingers tight around the frame surrounding the painting of Linden Street. She made a silent promise to Morton and Horatio and Leopold and Harvey, and to all the people who were still waiting inside of Elsewhere. Then she straightened her shoulders and headed into her bedroom.

Inside, she found Morton wriggling out of the scorched remains of the trench coat. Leopold, Harvey, and Horatio sat on the pillows, watching him. Their eyes flickered to Olive as she came in.

"I think we will spend the night at Morton's house, miss," said Leopold. "If you have no further need of us, that is."

"No," said Olive. "That's a good idea. I'm glad he'll have company."

Harvey stuck his paint-splotched head out into the hallway. "The corridor is unguarded," he whispered back into the room. "We must make our move."

Bumping each other out of the way, Harvey and Leopold stole through the bedroom door. Morton trailed after them, carrying the blue corduroy horse. He didn't look up as he passed the spot where Olive stood, not even when she put her hand on his arm. But he did stop walking.

"Morton," she whispered, "I'm sorry that things were how they were. I mean, I wish everything could have been different for you. I wish I could have made them different. I wish . . . I wish tonight didn't have to happen. I wish none of it ever had to happen."

Morton dropped his head. Olive couldn't tell if this was meant to be a nod, or if he was only staring down at the carpet. But then he turned to look at her over his shoulder, and his eyes met hers.

"I don't want to quit trying," he said firmly. "I don't want *you* to quit." Then, without another word, he slipped out into the hallway. Horatio and Olive were left alone.

"I'm scared, Horatio," Olive whispered, the doubts creeping back. "I don't feel safe here anymore."

"You're not," Horatio answered. He dropped gracefully to the floor, his orange bulk alighting without a sound. "But you've got us on your side. Remember that."

After a cautionary glance in all directions, Horatio slipped into the hallway. By the time Olive stepped out after him, he too had disappeared into the painting of Linden Street.

Olive stood in her open bedroom door. The house creaked and shifted around her, buffeted by the evening wind. The dark hallway dwindled away in two directions. From below her came the sound of her parents' voices and the clinking of dishes, carried on a soft wave of cooking smells. Olive walked slowly back down the staircase and into the light.

The dining room chandelier was glowing cheerily. Mrs. Dunwoody let Olive light the candles on the table, and the three Dunwoodys sat down together. The darkness outside closed over the windows like velvet curtains. Olive couldn't see through the pane. All she could see, when she looked at the glass, was the reflection of her own little family gathered around the table, passing each other the steaming dishes, all safe and sound inside, smiling as though everything was right with the world. It would be so easy to believe that everything *was* right.

Up and down Linden Street, a few brown petals were beginning to drop from summer flowers. Leaves rustled softly in the trees. Lamps glowed cozily behind closed curtains. The first edge of autumn hung in the breeze that whispered across porches and stoops, knocking gently at closed doors. And somewhere out there, in the darkness, Annabelle McMartin was free again.

Turn the page for a preview of
the next Book of Elsewhere.

VOLUME 3 IN THE *NEW YORK TIMES* BESTSELLING SERIES

THE BOOKS OF
ELSEWHERE

The
Second Spy
Jacqueline West

IF YOU BELIEVE that death is about to spring upon you at any moment, you won't spend much time watching television. You won't devote a lot of thought to bathing or tooth-brushing, either. Even things you once enjoyed, like reading, doodling, or daydreaming, will slide right off of your daily to-do list.

If you believe that death is coming for you, you'll do a lot of jumping around corners. You'll turn on all the lights in every room you enter, even on bright August afternoons. You will get surprisingly good at walking backward up staircases. You will never forget—not even for a minute—that doom could be waiting just through any doorway.

Your life will revolve between two things: spending as much time as possible with those you care about, and *hiding*.

Fortunately for Olive Dunwoody, who was whiling away the end of the summer in this particularly uncomfortable situation, she had the perfect way to do both.

Each morning, as soon as her parents were busy with their own work and worries, Olive put on the pair of antique spectacles that hung from a ribbon around her neck. Then she stepped from her bedroom into the hallway of the old stone house on Linden Street and watched the paintings that lined its walls ripple into life.

Painted grass waved in an intangible wind. Painted trees twitched. Painted people moved and blinked and stared back at her from the other side of their canvases.

Grabbing the edges of the picture frame that hung just outside her bedroom door, Olive would squish herself through the wavering, jelly-like surface, fall with a flop into the misty field, and bolt up the painted hill to find her friend Morton.

Morton was nine years old. He had been nine years old for a lot longer than eleven-year-old Olive had been eleven. In fact, he'd been nine years old for longer than Olive had been alive.

An old man's lifetime ago, Morton had lived with his family right next door to the old stone house on Linden Street. No one who lived right next door could have helped but notice something odd about the place . . . and about the McMartin family, who lived in it. Finally, the day had come when Morton's family knew too much.

Aldous McMartin, the painter and patriarch of the McMartin family, got rid of Morton by trapping him inside a painting. Morton's sister, Lucinda Nivens, who had hoped to be accepted into the McMartin family and taught their magical secrets, had eventually been betrayed and killed by the people she served. As for Morton's parents, they had vanished. No one knew where.

Well . . . not *no one*.

Annabelle McMartin knew.

But she wasn't about to tell.

To begin with, Annabelle McMartin was dead. She'd finally croaked at the age of 104, the last twisted twig on the McMartin family tree. Because she had died without an heir, all of the McMartin family treasures were left to clutter the corners and hang from the walls of their old stone house on Linden Street. The inconvenience of being dead should have kept Annabelle and her ancestors from causing anyone any trouble. But that was not the case. Not in *this* case. For among the many odd, dusty relics the McMartins had left behind were their portraits—magical, living, conniving portraits, painted by Aldous and craftily hidden in the house's depths. These portraits wanted nothing more than to take their house, with all its secrets and powers and history, *back*.

Olive had discovered this in the most unpleasant of ways.

The knowledge that the living painting of her home's former owner was on the loose, intent on revenge, was what had Olive jumping around corners and backing up staircases. Sometimes her eyes played tricks on her, and she would catch the flash of a painted tendril of long brown hair in the gleam of a wooden banister, or the sheen of a string of pearls floating above an empty chair. Annabelle's too-sweet, too-still smile seemed to glitter from the shadows of the house's darkened rooms.

This usually happened when Olive was alone.

Olive tried to be alone as little as possible.

When she was with Morton, she felt a bit less frightened. Her fear seemed to spread out between them, like a dose of awful medicine divided into two spoons. Together, Olive and Morton would slip through the creaking, cluttered rooms, climbing in and out of Elsewhere. They searched painting after painting for some sign of Morton's parents. They questioned every painted person they met. They flipped over every painted rock (the rocks always flipped themselves hurriedly upright again), they peered inside painted windows, and they peeped through the keyholes of painted doors. But when every rock had been flipped and every keyhole had been peeped, they still hadn't found a single new clue.

Fortunately, the search mixed some fun into the frustration. Sometimes Olive and Morton visited the painting of a ruined castle, where a painted porter happily led them on tour after tour. They scattered chubby pigeons on a painted Paris sidewalk. They clambered through the frame of a painted ballroom and danced to the music of the out-of-practice orchestra. If the house's kitchen was deserted, they dove into its painting of three stonemasons and played with Baltus, the large, shaggy dog that Olive had rescued from another painting. When they were feeling especially brave, they even went boating on the smooth silver lake where Annabelle had once left Olive to drown.

Often, one of the house's three guardian cats would accompany them. Olive would spot the spark of green eyes in the distance, across the painted waves of a river or between the brush-stroked petals of a blooming garden, and she would feel her fear spread even thinner, knowing that the cats were watching over her.

But nothing could lift the fear away completely.

And as the last days of summer tiptoed past, something else was creeping up on Olive. Something that swelled and darkened like a bruise in the back of her mind. Something even bigger and blacker and chillier than her own untimely and quite-possibly-impending death.

Junior high.

A FAMOUS POET ONCE wrote that April is the cruelest month. Olive knew this because she had come across the poem somewhere in the dusty library of the old stone house on Linden Street. She hadn't understood most of the poem, but she remembered the line about April. She remembered it because it was so obviously untrue. Olive knew—as all kids know—that the cruelest month is September. One morning, you wake up to a sky that still feels like a summer sky, and a breeze that still feels like a summer breeze, and you smile, looking forward to a whole day of freedom—and then your mother shouts up the stairs that you're already running fifteen minutes late, and if you don't get a move on, you'll miss the school bus.

This was just what happened to Olive. Except she didn't wake up looking forward to a day of freedom and adventure. She woke up exhausted, with a cramp in her legs from a night of dreams about a furious witch chasing her around and around a giant hamster wheel. As she squeezed Hershel, her worn brown bear, Olive told herself that these had been nothing but nightmares. The problem was, except for the giant hamster wheel bit, Olive's nightmares might come true.

"Olive!" Mrs. Dunwoody called from the foot of the stairs. "You're now seventeen point five minutes late and counting!"

With a sigh, Olive tucked Hershel back under the covers. She stood up in bed, wavering for a moment on the squishy mattress, and then jumped as far away from the bed as she could get without crashing into another piece of furniture. Olive did this every morning, just in case something with long, grabbing, painted arms was waiting underneath the bed. From several feet away, she bent down to check under the dust ruffle. No Annabelle. Olive opened her closet with a practiced yank-and-leap-backward maneuver. This way, if Annabelle were indeed waiting inside, Olive would be hidden behind the door. She peeped through the door frame. No Annabelle. Olive tugged on a clean shirt, carefully arranging the spectacles inside the collar, and hustled out into the hallway.

Even on clear September mornings, the upstairs hall of the old stone house remained shadowy and dim. Faint rays of sun glinted on the paintings that lined the walls. Olive's fingers gave a twitch. The temptation to put on the spectacles and dive into Elsewhere tugged at her like a strand of hair caught in a rusty zipper.

"Olive!" called Mrs. Dunwoody. "There are just thirty-four minutes until the school day begins!"

With a last longing glance over her shoulder, Olive headed for the stairs, slipped on the top step, and just managed to catch herself on the banister before toppling rump-over-teakettle down the staircase.

Because it was Olive's very first day of junior high school, Mr. Dunwoody had fixed a special pancake breakfast. Mrs. Dunwoody kissed Olive on the head and told her how grown-up she looked. Then Mr. Dunwoody made her pose for a photograph on the front porch holding her book bag and her fancy graphing calculator, and after that, Mrs. Dunwoody drove her to school because she had already missed the bus and if she walked she *would* have been tardy by more than fifteen minutes. And yet neither of her parents noticed that Olive (whose brain was even more distracted than usual) was still wearing her pink penguin pajama bottoms with ruffles across the seat of the pants.

But the kids at school did.

Everyone in Olive's homeroom laughed so loudly that students walking down the hall stopped to see what was so funny. One boy laughed until his face turned the color of kidney beans, and he had to go to the nurse's office to use his asthma inhaler.

A girl with long, dark hair and a sharp nose—a girl who, Olive noticed, was wearing *eyeliner*—leaned across the aisle to Olive's desk. "They're mean, aren't they?" she asked. "Don't worry about them," the girl went on as Olive tried to squeeze out an answer. "I think your pants are *adorable*." Here the girl raised her voice a little bit, so that everyone around them could hear. "But didn't you know that the *kindergarten* is in another building?"

All the kids went off on another roar of laughter, and Olive wished she could sink down into the cracks in the floor with the eraser scrapings and pencil dust.

The morning didn't get any better. During her second class, when the students were supposed to stand up and tell about themselves, Olive mumbled that she was eleven, that her parents were both math professors, that her family had moved to town at the beginning of summer, and—because she couldn't think of anything else to say—that she had a birth-mark shaped very much like a pig right above her belly button, which was true, but which she certainly hadn't planned to admit to anyone.

During her third class, Olive asked to go to the restroom and got so lost afterward that she wandered around the building for almost an hour and wound up in a storage room behind the gymnasium, where a friendly janitor finally found her.

When lunchtime came, Olive tiptoed into the cafeteria with a fleet of butterflies doing death-spirals in her stomach. The tables were already crowded with students (Olive had gotten lost on the way to the cafeteria too), and everyone was shouting and laughing and stealing food from one another's trays. She blinked around, wondering how she was ever going to feel brave enough to sit down at one of those tables, and whether it would be dangerously unsanitary for her to take her lunch back to the rest-room and eat it there, when, like one stalled car in a sea of roaring traffic, a quiet table surfaced amid the chaos.

The table was empty except for one rumpled boy. A boy with smudgy glasses, and messy brown hair, and a large blue dragon on his shirt.

Large blue dragons had never looked friendlier. Olive made a beeline for the table.

"Hi, Rutherford," she said, smiling for the first time all day.

Rutherford Dewey glanced up. Before Olive had even had time to plop into a chair, he asked, "Have you heard about the pliosaur skull that was discovered on the Jurassic coast?"

There were several questions Olive could have asked in response to this. ("Where's the Jurassic coast?" "What's a plierssaur?" "Is that its name because it looks like a pair of pliers?") But the only answer she could give was "No." So she gave it.

"It's a fascinating find," Olive's neighbor went on, in a rapid, slightly nasal voice that was only partially muffled by a mouthful of chicken salad. "The skull itself is nearly eight feet long. The pliosaur's entire body probably measured around fifty feet, which is more than twice the size of an orca."

"An orca is a killer whale, right?" asked Olive, unwrapping her sandwich.

"Yes, although the name 'killer whale' is a bit unfair. The orca isn't an especially murderous creature. Besides, all of us are killers of *something*."

"No we're—" Olive cut herself off mid-argument, wondering if dissolving something evil that came out of a painting counted as "killing."

Rutherford watched her take the first bite. "What's that in your sandwich?" he asked.

"Peanut butter."

"Then you're a peanut killer. It's inevitable. Each of us has to kill to survive."

Olive squirmed. For the hundredth time that day, she touched the lump of the spectacles underneath her shirt, making sure they were still there.

"Don't worry," said Rutherford. "My grandmother will be keeping a very close watch on the neighborhood while we're at school. She'll be watching your house especially."

Olive glanced up into Rutherford's intent brown eyes. Not for the first time, she had the strange feeling that Rutherford must have been reading her mind. Of course, she reminded herself, it wouldn't be hard for him to *guess* what she was worrying about.

"Your grandmother hasn't seen any sign of . . . of *Annabelle,* has she?" Olive asked, dropping her voice to a whisper.

Rutherford shook his head, looking unconcerned. He looked just as unconcerned a second later, when a wad of plastic wrap sailed through the air and beaned him on the head. "No. No sign of her presence," he went on as a group of boys at a table nearby slapped each other's hands and sniggered. "And my grandmother has also placed a protective charm on your house, which prevents anyone who isn't invited inside from entering the house itself. She uses the same kind of charm on ours. It dates back to the middle ages, when it was placed on the walls of castles and fortresses, and thus it doesn't protect outdoor spaces; however, it is still quite effective." Noticing that Olive's eyes were beginning to glaze, Rutherford changed the subject. "Have you heard about Mrs. Nivens?"

Olive almost inhaled a chunk of sandwich. She looked around, making sure no one else had heard. "What about her?"

"The police have declared her a missing person. They've searched her house and everything. Now it's locked up and they're keeping it under surveillance."

Olive put down her sandwich. "I don't think they'll figure out what really happened. Do you?"

One of Rutherford's eyebrows went up. "You mean, that Mrs. Nivens was actually a magical painting trying to serve a family of dead witches, one of whom finally turned on her?" The eyebrow came down again. "I think it's highly unlikely."

"Yeah." Olive paused. "They sure won't figure it out from looking around her house. Everything is so *normal.*" Olive's mind darted back to the evening when she, Morton, and the cats had tiptoed through the eerily clean and quiet rooms of Mrs. Nivens's house—a house that had hidden Mrs. Nivens's secret for nearly a century.

A not-quite-empty carton of milk hit the center

of their table, exploding in a fountain of tepid white droplets. The boys at the nearby table guffawed.

"It's been my experience that those people who seem the most 'normal' are in fact the most dangerous," said Rutherford, wiping a drip of milk off the end of his nose.

Olive dragged her penguin-dotted legs through the rest of the afternoon. She spent science class staring at the shelves of beakers and test tubes, remembering the chamber full of strange, murky jars that she'd found beneath the basement of the old stone house, and missing half of the instructions for the very first assignment. Next, she spent history class thinking about all the people Aldous McMartin had trapped inside his paintings, becoming so absorbed that she didn't hear the teacher calling on her until he'd said her name three times. But the minutes ticked by, and the last hour of the day crawled closer, and finally, Olive found herself climbing the stairs to the third floor and trudging along the hall to the art classroom.

Olive pulled up a metal stool to a high white table as far away from all the other students as she could get. Then she waited.

And waited.

And waited.